ZEKE

HOLLIISTER
BOOK 2

KRIS MICHAELS

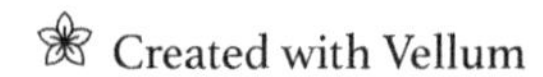
Created with Vellum

1

"You don't think I broke it, do you? Mom does, but I don't. I mean, there's no bone or anything sticking out." Flynn Esteves looked up at him, his eyes pleading with Zeke.

"You fell fifteen feet," his mother grumbled, "It's broken."

Doctor Ezekiel Johnson smiled and placed the young boy's arm in the correct position so he could take an x-ray. The new machine Guardian had installed for him now that he was assisting Adam Cassidy with the population that worked at the ranch was a Godsend and light-years ahead of the archaic machine he'd kept on life support for the last five years.

"Why were you up in a tree in the middle of winter?" He'd seen Flynn several times over the years. He kept his mom, a single mother who worked in the school's office, hopping; that was for sure.

"Well ..." He glanced over at his mother.

"Go ahead, tell him." She waved and headed out the door. "I'm going to go wash my hands."

Flynn looked back at him and opened his mouth to speak, but Zeke held up a hand. "Hold that thought. Don't move." He ducked behind the protective wall and hit the button on the computer to capture the image. Then he returned to reposition the arm. "Okay, how?" he asked as he moved Flynn's arm position.

"I was mad at Mom for saying I couldn't drive the snowmobile. So I was going to hide out in my treehouse, you know, to give us both some space."

Zeke made a face. "Dude, in the winter? That's just wrong. She would have been so worried if she couldn't find you."

Flynn deflated. "Yeah. That's what she said, and I get it, but, Doc Zeke." He looked up at Zeke. "Sometimes, she smothers me. I'm almost thirteen, and she treats me like I'm two."

Zeke chuckled as he walked back behind the wall. “Can I let you in on a secret? Don’t move.”

Flynn froze and barely moved his lips as he spoke. “Sure, lay it on me.”

“Everyone’s mom treats them like they’re still their baby. Mine does, and I’m forty-two.”

Flynn groaned. “You mean there’s no hope?”

Zeke took the image and laughed. “You get used to it. Believe me. Maybe next time, explain to your mom that you’re almost a teenager and why you feel like she’s smothering you.”

“You say that like she’d listen.” Flynn rolled his eyes.

“I’d listen,” Gia Esteves said from the doorway. “I might not change my mind, but I’d listen. You getting older is hard on both of us. Talk to me next time, and if I don’t listen, say ‘treehouse,’ and I’ll either stop and try to understand you or explain why my concerns prevent me from allowing you to do what you want.”

“Well, that sounds practical.” Zeke motioned to them. “I’ll be right back. I need to look at the images.”

Zeke walked out of the room and damn near ran into Jeremiah Wheeler. His friend and fellow doctor in the small clinic was supposed to be home. "Hey, what are you doing back here?" He glanced down the hall. "Eden and the kids with you?" They fell into step as they walked to the office area of the clinic.

"No, I have a conference call with the big wigs at Guardian and didn't want to be interrupted, so I came in. That was some good advice you dispensed back there." Jeremiah leaned against the door frame as Zeke headed to his PC.

"I remember struggling with my mom. She raised me by herself." Zeke started his computer and waited for it to boot up.

"I thought ... but your dad?" Jeremiah stepped into Zeke's office and closed the door.

"Pete? He's my stepdad and married Mom when I left for college. I've never had anyone else, so I call him Dad." Zeke shrugged and navigated through the programs to get to the imagery of Flynn's arm.

"Didn't know that. Hey, did you get dinner, or have you been here all night?"

"I haven't left yet. Wallace isn't doing well. Dillon Bradshaw is with him now. I'll go out as soon as I get Flynn ..." Zeke looked at the different views of the x-ray and continued, "a cast. Clean break."

"I'm sorry." Jeremiah put a hand on his shoulder. "If you need to talk about it, let me know."

"Thanks, but I'm good." He'd sat with dying patients before. The least he could do was keep his patient comfortable until the inevitable happened.

"Offer stands. I have to go sign in. Anything you want me to pass on?"

Zeke chuckled. "Thank them again for the new equipment, and let them know I'm available if they need me."

"Believe me, Adam sure as hell appreciates it. With the scale back out there, he's alone and on-call twenty-four-seven."

Guardian Security was recovering from a terrorist attack. But, while the company might have been down, it wasn't out. Zeke had seen the organization's resilience firsthand and witnessed the clean-up and repair of the ranch where Guardian had a training center. There was no doubt the company would find a way to recover. "They'll rebuild."

"Eventually. I think management at Guardian is strategically targeting where and when. Triage, if you will." Jeremiah opened the door that led to his office.

"Smart is what it is." Zeke put his computer to sleep and headed down the hall. "Yo, Flynn, your mom was right. What color cast do you want? I've got blue, purple, or red."

Zeke leaned back in the worn leather chair that was pulled up beside the old single bed. The mattress was probably older than Zeke, and the divot pressed through the padding was formed into the shape of the old man lying beside him.

Wallace Lamont had lived a long life. So long that he'd outlived his wife and children. As Zeke listened to his raspy breathing, he glanced around the small room in the two-hundred-year-old farmhouse. An old black and white picture of Wallace and his wife hung on the wall. Another showed him, his wife, and his two sons. Both sons were taken from him during a war fought on foreign soil. Wallace never said which war.

At ninety-seven, he'd slipped and fallen getting out of the shower. Dillon Bradshaw, Wallace's neighbor, who stopped by every morning for coffee and to see if Wallace needed anything, had found him. The resulting injuries, although not severe, had been a precursor to the beginning of Wallace's end.

Maybe he would take Jeremiah up on that talk. Losing Wallace meant losing a part of their town. He'd become a permanent fixture outside Sanderson's grocery store from spring through early fall on

Saturdays. The cooler weather was tough on his bones, so he and his ever-shrinking circle of friends migrated to Gen's diner when it grew cold. There, they'd listen to the "old hens" cackling about the town's business.

Zeke smiled. Truth be told, Wallace and his friends knew more about what was going on than those old women. Everyone knew Wallace Lamont. He had a kind word and a ready smile for everyone.

"You don't need to be here for this, doc." Wallace coughed.

"I have nowhere else I want to be. You've always been good to me, Wallace. You've been good to everyone."

"Nora's doing. She was better than me by a long shot. Trained me up." Another round of coughing ended their conversation for a while. When Zeke had finally convinced Wallace to go to Belle Fourche for follow-up, subsequent to his diagnosis of bruised ribs, the doctors did a blood workup and then a scan. It showed the cancer that was killing Wallace. Another scan in Rapid proved the disease had metastasized to most of his organs. Wallace chose to go home and die where he'd lived.

"Nora sounds like a wonderful woman."

Wallace made a noise of agreement. "The best.

You're young. You need to find yourself a woman to love." His voice was a mere whisper.

Zeke snorted out a small laugh. "I'm forty-two. I've done the dating game and have pretty much given up on it. Medicine takes all my time anyway." He'd been burned, spurned, and returned. He wasn't sure if he would open that can of worms again. Those days, he worked for Hollister and Guardian, went home, puttered with his projects, and used the new addition he'd built onto his house as a gym. He concentrated on himself during the downtime. Lonely? Sure, but it was better than the ups and downs of dating. He figured he was meant to be a bachelor.

"Nobody should go through life alone," Wallace said with his eyes shut. He was struggling.

Zeke kept talking to him to let him know he was there. "I'm not alone. I have my friends." Which was true. The little town of Hollister didn't have many residents, but through his work, he'd made friends in the town and on the surrounding ranches that would last a lifetime.

He stared down at the man and listened as he coughed and released a soft moan. Wallace opened his eyes a sliver and stared up at him. "Not the same.

I'm dying. Got no time for niceties. Find yourself a woman or a man and love them."

Zeke smiled and patted the bony weathered hand of a man who'd lived almost a hundred years. "I prefer women."

"Knew two or three that didn't. Live and let live." Wallace stared at the photo of his family across the room. "Had a good life. I miss them." A tear slipped from Wallace's eye.

"You have had a wonderful life," Zeke agreed. Wallace nodded once, sighed, and closed his eyes.

Six hours later, without any resuscitation, as was his wish, Wallace Lamont, ninety-seven, and a life-long resident of Hollister, South Dakota, took his last breath. Zeke closed his eyes and said a prayer, and then he looked out the window at the slowly graying winter sunrise. "Say hello to Nora and your sons for me, Wallace."

Zeke placed the call to the funeral home that Wallace had chosen. He picked up the packet of papers beside Wallace's bed and opened it as instructed. A Last Will and Testament and several letters addressed to various residents of Hollister were inside. Zeke had promised he'd deliver them. While he waited for the funeral home to make the trip from

Belle Fourche, Zeke went about the administrative side of a patient passing, which included notifications and filling out Wallace's death certificate. His birth certificate was in the packet. Zeke carefully opened the fragile paper, transcribed the required information, and put the document back into the pouch.

The funeral home arrived, and Zeke waited for them to remove Wallace before he cleaned up the single bed, removing the soiled bedding and picking up the detritus of managed end-of-life care. Zeke turned down the heat but ensured it remained warm enough in the small home, so the pipes didn't freeze. He put his equipment into his truck and stared at the little house. Would that be his ending? Alone? He stared down at the steering wheel and drew a deep breath. No, Wallace wasn't alone. He shook his head. Morbid thoughts for a cold morning. A wave of exhaustion rolled over him as he put the truck into gear and headed back to the office.

As he turned off the highway, the trucks lined in front of Gen's diner beckoned to him. The need for community at a time of loss was strong, at least for him. He pulled into a vacant slot and trudged through the snow to the diner door. He ducked through the door, and the entire place quieted as everyone looked at him. He shook his head.

Reverend Campbell cleared his throat. "Can we lower our heads for a moment?" Zeke closed his eyes and stood respectfully as the reverend said a blessing for Wallace. When he was done, Zeke looked for a place to sit.

"Here you go, Doc, we got room," Tegan Wells called over to him. The manager of the local stockyard slid deeper into the booth.

Zeke headed over and thanked Tegan before he nodded to Carson Schmidt, the man who ran Hollister's hardware store.

"Long night," Carson said. It was spoken as a fact, not a question, so Zeke just nodded.

Ciera Evers, newly married and radiantly happy, brought him a cup of coffee. "Breakfast?"

He shook his head. "Just coffee this morning."

"Sorry to hear about Wallace. He was a good man." Ciera put her hand on Zeke's shoulder.

"He was," Zeke agreed before she left.

"You got your plans drawn up for the garage you wanted to add onto the house?" Carson took a bite of his biscuit.

Zeke appreciated the change of subject. "Plans? Just thought I'd frame it out and build it." He'd done exactly that when he'd built his addition the previous year.

Tegan chuckled. "Sounds about right. Got no time for engineers and such. I added my porch last year. Cement blocks stacked to floor level tied them to the house with some foot-long bolts and lugs, framed it up, slapped on the decking, and done. Took two weekends."

"You built that house, didn't you, Tegan?" Zeke took a sip of his coffee. Strong and delicious.

"I did. But I'll admit I pulled the plans off the internet for that. Needed to make sure I wasn't going to mess it up. I also made the outside walls thicker, so I could stuff way too much insulation in there. But I tell you, the fire in my fireplace can keep that house warm if necessary." Tegan popped the rest of his cinnamon roll into his mouth.

"Not sure how much more to put into the house after the garage." Zeke had renovated that little place as much as he could. Starting over seemed a waste of time and energy.

"You'll find other projects. We all do." Tegan shrugged and took a drink of his coffee.

"If you were hitched, you'd have even more to do." Carson chuckled.

Tegan snorted. "Carson, I smell of stockyard, and I work all the time. When am I going to find someone?"

"Amen." Zeke lifted his coffee cup.

Tegan glanced at him and lifted an eyebrow. "Just what exactly are you agreeing to?"

"To working all the time. Why?"

"He thought you were agreeing to him smelling like a stockyard." Carson laughed so hard that he drew the attention of the rest of the diner.

Tegan threw his napkin on the plate. "Listen here, Carson."

"More coffee?" Ciera slid up to the table with a pot in her hand.

"Please." All three lifted their cups for her.

"Doc, you sure I can't get you something?" Ciera took Tegan's plate as she spoke.

"I'm sure. I'm going to head home and fall into a coma for about eight hours after I finish this cup."

"You'd sleep better with food in your stomach. Just saying."

He chuckled. "Okay. A sausage biscuit, please."

A smile split Ciera's face, and she almost danced back to the kitchen.

"Damn, she's changed." Tegan nodded in Ciera's direction. "Marriage agrees with her."

"Seems to," Zeke agreed. He knew a few of the particulars of her story because of his work with

Guardian. Enough that he was pleased the woman and her son were happy and safe.

Carson rolled his eyes. “We’re all confirmed bachelors.”

Tegan took a sip of his coffee. “Nothing wrong with that.”

Zeke smiled and tuned back into the conversation between his friends. He finished his coffee, ate the biscuit that Ciera brought him, and excused himself. He needed sleep.

2

Stephanie Howard was awake long before she heard the laughter outside the door. The flash of Declan's headlights had illuminated the corner of the living room where she'd been huddled since her nightmare had awakened her. She lifted her eyes to the door and groaned at the sight of her brother and one of his women plastered against the decorative frosted glass window in the center of the front door. She slid back under the blankets piled on the sofa as Declan fumbled with the doorknob.

Would it be wrong to send up a small prayer asking that the woman wasn't a howler like the last one? She really needed to start work on the old farmhouse. It was an idea she'd mentioned to

Declan a time or two since she'd decided to stay in Hollister. She hadn't told anyone she'd be staying. Not that anyone but Declan would care. She hadn't been to town in months and assumed no one had missed her. Not like she was the toast of the town. Though, that opinion was partially her fault.

Anyway, she and Declan needed their own spaces, and cleaning out the old place was the perfect solution because, right then, Hollister was the best place for her to be, and that ... well, that was a wickedly hard pill to swallow.

Even so, the old place needed a lot of love and cleaning before it was habitable. At least she'd be able to ramble around in the house during the middle of the night without waking her brother or his frequent overnight guests. Living with Declan was like living in a house with a revolving door. A new girl every weekend, sometimes during the week, too. Sure, her brother was good-looking and had a business, which made him even more attractive to some women, but listening to her brother boink every piece of strange he brought home was an audio nightmare. It was a miracle he hadn't run out of women. Maybe he had? Maybe he was working through the eligible women again. Stephanie shuddered at the thought.

She waited as the woman giggled herself and her brother through the front room. Thankfully, the convertible couch where she slept was out of the main traffic path. She didn't need company to fall into her bed accidentally. The door to the only bedroom slammed closed, and the woman's gasp of pleasure was her cue to move. Steph pushed the quilt off and headed to the kitchen.

Wincing at the sudden illumination of the overhead light, she blinked until she could see and grabbed an oversized yellow ceramic mug out of the cupboard. She put the kettle on the burner and turned on the outside light. Through the dim yellow glow, she could almost see the outline of the old ranch house she and Declan had grown up in. It had been vacant since Declan had built his house when she was in college.

The shrill whistle of the kettle sounded, and she hustled over to the stove to turn off the burner. Steph poured the hot water over her tea bag. Letting it steep, she sat at the table and carefully examined the rolled-up bottoms of Declan's sweatpants. She was wearing his sweatshirt, too.

Her current state of less than haute couture, sans makeup, and messy hair would have sent her ex, Presley, off the deep end. She shuddered at the thought of his anger. The psychological and physical abuse she'd suffered at his hands lived adjacent to her daily thoughts. A caution that seemed to linger and taint every interaction she had with people. Had. Declan had been her only company for months.

She pulled the tea bag out, pressing it between her fingers before throwing it in the garbage and taking a sip of the cinnamon-flavored herbal tea. Presley had probably looked for her, although with each passing day, she'd started to breathe easier. The cash she'd taken out of her account the morning she'd disappeared was dwindling quickly, and she'd have to find a job. Of course, Declan told her she could work at the bar, but she didn't want to be in the center of a bunch of drunk men. Although the entire town thought she had, she hadn't cheated on Andrew Hollister. Mack Jensen spread horrible rumors about her, and then Donna Franks started repeating it as if it were gospel. True, she'd figured out she didn't love Andrew, but the evil and pervasive gossip Donna had spread made her out to be wicked and unfaithful. Any conversation she had with a man turned into her sleeping around.

She'd examined the way things had gone down. She and Andrew had dated forever. He'd been at both funeral services for her parents. The entire town expected them to marry. It was a given—except they didn't love each other. He was a friend, and they'd experimented with sex. When Andrew left for college and then the service, she'd grown up, and so had he. Should she have sent him a Dear John letter? Maybe. The night Mack Jenson had tried to have sex with her, she'd kneed him in the balls and told him she'd tell the town he'd tried to rape her. Only Mack and his aunt Donna had other ideas. They attacked her before she could say a word. When she'd tried to defend herself, Mack's version was already around town. No one believed her, and everyone felt sorry for Andrew. Mack was also Ken Zorn's second cousin, which also complicated things. Ken was a good friend of Andrew's. That period in her life had been miserable. Or, at least, she'd thought it had been. Now? Not so much.

She took a sip of her tea and stared out the window at the snowflakes as they fluttered through the light of the small bulb illuminating the porch. The repetitive thudding of the headboard against the wall earned an eye roll from her. If she went by the sounds alone, her brother was a sex god. And ewww, that was something she never wanted to think about again. A long moan and a rapid percussion followed. See? Sex God. She sighed. She shook her head, knowing sounds of enjoyment could be faked. Everything could be faked.

Stephanie sighed and stared at her nails. She'd popped off the fake overlays a couple of weeks after arriving in Hollister and kept her natural nails filed down. Presley would have been appalled. She had to always look her best for him, and the stubby nails would have earned her a berating or maybe a beating. Stephanie bit her bottom lip. She had to look good enough to impress his "clients and associates." His exact words. She remembered the day a week before she'd fled. He'd held her hair, pulling her to her feet from the tile floor where he'd shoved her. "You stupid bitch. Why do I keep you around? What good are you to me? I should let my boys have a turn with you. Let you see how good you have it. Maybe then you'd appreciate me." Then he'd backhanded her across the cheek.

A tear slipped down her cheek, and she batted it away. Everything Presley had was a possession, including her. She'd learned to apply makeup to cover bruises, smile even though her lip was cut or swollen, and move when the bruises under her clothes made her ache for the comfort of a bed.

Tears flowed down her cheek unchecked as she

tried to remember when things had become so horrible. Presley had been so charming at first. Attentive and kind, he wooed her as if she was the most beautiful woman he'd ever seen. She'd been so in love with him. He treated her as if she was irreplaceable and precious. It wasn't the high school romance she and Andrew shared. There was passion, and she thought there was love. But all too soon, she'd learned she wasn't a person to Presley. She was an object to acquire, control, and use.

Lord, how hadn't she seen the manipulation? The way he'd removed her from the circle of friends she'd found in Denver was so ... slick. She hadn't even recognized it until it was too late. The isolation, the manipulation, and the lies. But by the time she opened her eyes to what was happening, she'd become a prisoner in a gilded cage. A cage bought and paid for with drug money, but the bars were constructed with her embarrassment. She couldn't go home. She'd left in disgrace. Going back to Hollister wasn't possible until it became her only choice.

She may have been a stupid object to Presley, but she listened and understood what she'd heard. Cocaine, meth, and oxy were Presley's business. The bespoke clothes and mansion in the finest suburb of

Denver were window dressings to make him look respectable.

The morning she'd left him had been a freak opportunity she had to take. One of Presley's men had brought the loaner Mercedes back and left the keys to the vehicle on the kitchen counter. Presley and his security team weren't home, but they were due back shortly. The front door's alarm had been deactivated by the man who brought the car back, and when he left, there was no tell-tale chirp of the system going back on. She waited until the man reached the SUV that had trailed him into the gated compound, and when the vehicle left, she checked the door. Not armed. Presley wouldn't be notified that she'd opened the door. No security, no alarm to announce her leaving, and transportation away from the bastard.

Stephanie flew into the room she occupied. Not Presley's room. She wasn't allowed there anymore. The clothes she'd hastily thrown into her suitcase and tossed into the Mercedes were a mish-mash of skirts and blouses. A smaller tote held her shoes and underwear, and she crammed her makeup and bathroom items into the spaces between her shoes' heels. She bolted out of the house, keys in hand, and fired up the vehicle. "Open, please open." She pressed in the code that Presley gave his men who used the Mercedes. It had never changed, and she prayed it still worked. The gate rolled back, and she drove away. The bank was her first stop. She withdrew all the money she had in her private account. Money Presley hadn't allowed her to access. After filling up the car, she drove in a crazy disjointed route all the way home.

Stephanie picked at the heavy gray sweat pant material that warmed her. Presley didn't think slacks or jeans were appropriate for his woman to wear. She didn't have the right clothes to live in Hollister, and she hadn't ordered anything because Presley's name was on her credit cards. She'd cut those up, so she wouldn't be tempted to use them since he could track her down if she did. It was also why the Mercedes was parked in the barn and covered with a tarp. Declan had helped her do that. And she supposed she'd involved him in a crime by asking him to help her, but she had nowhere else to go.

Months of soul searching, healing, and, yes, self-pity had drained her of the poison Presley had placed in her life. Well, most of the poison. She glanced out the window at the old place. She was ready. Ready to strike out on her own. To live again and to face the life she'd left in Hollister. Small steps.

She could do it, and she would. First, move into the old place. Second, get a job. Third ... Well, she didn't have a clue what the third step was, but she'd figure it out when the time came.

"Sorry we woke you."

Stephanie gasped and grabbed her chest. "Shit, Declan, you almost gave me a heart attack."

"I've been standing here awhile. Your tea's cold." He put the pot back on the stove.

"Is it?" Picking up the cup, she took a sip. Ice cold. "Huh. I guess I zoned out."

Declan stared at her. "What were you thinking about?"

Stephanie blinked up at him. "Ah, the old place. I think I'll go over and clean it out when it gets light."

"I guess I'm not the best roommate, am I?" He dropped into a chair beside her. Her big brother was her hero and always ran into battle to protect her. If he ever found out about Presley, he'd kill the man. And that was why she'd never tell him the truth about what had happened and why she'd returned home.

"If I were a frat boy, I'd probably worship you." She crumbled up her paper napkin and tossed it at him.

Catching the fluff, he launched it toward the

trash can, where it landed perfectly inside the container. "The heater might not work over there. It's only going to get colder."

She quickly calculated the money she had remaining in her wallet. "Do you think it's something major, or maybe we can patch it up?" She'd have to start working soon. There were a couple of options always open. The bar was the best solution, although the thought of working in that environment made her ill.

She'd tried so hard when she returned to be the woman they all expected her to be. To be the flirt, the woman on the hunt. It was just too damn hard. When you're beaten to the ground, pretending you're a strong, confident woman who didn't care what people thought of you was a tough stretch.

The day she'd driven into town, Edna had filled her full of information about Andrew's fiancée Gen. Immediately, Stephanie knew she had to introduce herself to Gen and wish them well. She was glad Andrew had found someone special, but Stephanie realized every old biddy at that table expected her to make a scene. But why? What had she ever done to make them think she was the type of person who would do that? Had the rumors multiplied or morphed after she'd left? For God's sake, they'd been friends all through high school. She hoped Gen would take care of him.

Portraying something she wasn't was too hard to keep doing. That was why she never went to town anymore. It had been months since she'd put on her armor, which was the word she associated with the makeup and the clothes Presley had bought her. She lived in Declan's sweats, cleaned his house, and cooked food for him to earn her keep. Although he never asked for it, she also gave him money for food.

"So you're staying." Declan stood up and grabbed the pot as it started to whistle.

She swallowed hard and nodded. "If that's okay?"

"You know this is your home. I was just waiting for you to make a choice to stay or go." He slid her the box of tea bags and emptied her cup before he poured hot water back into the mug. "I can look at the heater tomorrow before I go to work. I'll foot the cost of repair."

Stephanie jolted. "No, I'm not asking you to do that."

Declan sighed and dropped into the chair again. "Look, I don't know what happened to make you come home, but my gut is telling me whatever it was, was bad. You've been home almost six months, and you aren't the same person."

Steph straightened her shoulders. "What do you mean?"

"When you first came back, you tried. You got all fancied up and walked the walk, but you were scared. I know you. You couldn't hold onto that fuck-you attitude. That's why you stopped going into town. They didn't notice, but I did."

"I think you're imagining things." She clenched her hands to keep them from shaking.

Declan leaned forward and shook his head. "I'm not. You wake up with nightmares. I've heard you cry out, so don't deny it. Plus, you jump when I move too fast and always say sorry. You walk around on eggshells. Hell, the only time you haven't acted like someone beat the crap out of you is when you got all dolled up, but even that couldn't hold you together, could it?"

Shrugging, she looked down. "I know. I've been getting up the nerve to make an appointment with Doctor Wheeler. But I need a job first. I don't know how much that will cost." She couldn't counter anything he'd said. She'd lied enough. Maybe it was time to start over. To become the woman she wished she could have become all those years ago when she'd left that two-horse town.

Declan leaned forward. "Steph, whatever

happened to you has driven you back to the place you said you'd never come back to."

She carefully opened the tea bag's little paper jacket and placed the mesh bag into the hot water. Then she lifted and dropped the pouch several times until it sank. Finally, she cleared her throat. "I'm not leaving. If I can clean the old place up and you don't mind me living there, I'll be fine. I'll talk to Doctor Wheeler. I promise."

"You can stay there or here, Steph, but I have to ask, why do you need to see Doc Wheeler?" Declan put his hand over hers. "What happened to you? Why did you hide your car, and what is Cheston Enterprises?"

Fear dropped her gut, and she swallowed hard, fighting back the panic that hit her like a tsunami jumbling her senses in a tumble of waves rolling her until she couldn't breathe. "Where did you hear that name?" How she got the oxygen into her lungs to say the words was beyond her comprehension.

"It's on the registration of the Mercedes. What is that? Did the man you were with in Denver hurt you? Are you in trouble?"

She pursed her lips and shook her head. "Declan, I swear to you I haven't done anything wrong."

"Then tell me what happened."

She shook her head. "No. I'm not ready." Man, that was the understatement of the decade.

"You know I can find him. There's an address on the registration." He crossed his arms over his chest, and the small kitchen chair groaned under his weight. The bulk of his muscled arms made his t-shirt scream for relief. Her brother could do some serious damage to Presley, but she'd never want him to touch the filth that Presley lived in. The filth she'd escaped.

She reached out and grabbed his arm. "Don't. I left him. It's over. I'm here. I'm not leaving."

"And the car?"

"That piece of shit can turn into rust and fall apart, or you can take it apart and fix that old car of Dad's with the parts."

Declan barked out a laugh. "Dad would roll over in his grave. I wouldn't put a Mercedes engine into a Chevy."

"Whatever. It just can never see the light of day again." She took a sip of her tea. "I don't want you involved. Just pretend it isn't there."

"Does he know where to look for you?" Declan asked in a deadly quiet tone, the one he used when raging mad.

"No. He never took that much interest in me." Which was as far from the truth as possible. He directed every minute of her life, but he didn't know where in South Dakota she was from. She'd been embarrassed about being a hick from Hollister and lied. She'd told him she grew up in Sioux Falls. She and Declan weren't close. Well, they weren't after she'd left. A couple of calls a year before Presley. Now, she wondered why she'd been so hell-bent on cutting herself off from him and the little town of Hollister. Hindsight was always twenty-twenty. She'd heard that saying all the time growing up. Understanding what it meant was a hard lesson, but she'd learned it.

"It's over?" Declan asked her, catching her gaze with his. He held the connection as he waited for an answer.

"Yes. It is. I left him. He may be mad about the car, but it was the oldest one he had, and he loaned it out to his employees all the time. He won't be looking for it or me for long. He'll buy a new car and find someone new." She shivered at the thought of the man finding someone else to abuse, but what could she do?

"Well, it doesn't have computer assist, so he wouldn't have been able to track it or you. We'll keep it in the barn covered up until we can think of something else to do with it. I'll get the heater fixed up over at the old place." He nodded in the direction of the house they'd grown up in. "I like having you here, Steph."

She smiled at him. "Believe it or not ... I never thought I'd say this, but I'm so glad to be back."

"Never say never, right?"

"It would seem." She watched as he stood and ambled out of the kitchen. The low, purred female voice she heard when he opened his bedroom door told her the headboard would get another workout. She slowly finished her tea and glanced at the clock as the rhythmic thudding started again. Sunup couldn't come fast enough.

STEPHANIE FED another log into the fireplace. She'd worked from first light, and the sun was fading on the horizon, but she'd done it. The downstairs of the old place was clean.

A sense of immense satisfaction washed over her. She'd done a good job. Presley would have found fault, but he always did. The question was what would make him angry enough to set him off. She never knew.

But he didn't belong here. She'd done well and was proud of herself as she gazed around her old home. The little battery-operated camping lanterns glowed and cast a golden hue across the hardwoods she'd scrubbed to a shine.

She'd dusted everything and beat the heck out of the large square carpet after tossing it over the clothesline. She'd watched her mom and grand-mother do it a hundred times, and it wasn't as fun or easy as they'd made it appear. Steph had to hold her breath as she swung the spiraled metal rod her grandpa had made for her grandmother to use. The dust and ... other stuff freed from the carpet was disgusting and made the white snow under it a brownish-gray sludge.

When she tired of beating on the carpet, she went back in and cleaned the kitchen, the bath-rooms, and the bedrooms. The upstairs was nothing but storage, so that could wait. After she was convinced the carpet held no other secrets or scary things and had been beaten into submission, she made her way back into the house. After twisting the mop in the press, she squeezed the last of the dirty water out of it, then placed the well-used mop in the washroom and lifted the bucket. "You're all that's left between me and being done." She laughed. "Steph, you are talking to the freaking bucket."

In her defense, Declan wasn't much of a conversationalist when he was down in the furnace room cussing at the old heater.

"Is it dead?" she asked when he emerged covered in grease and dirt.

"Dead? Not quite. I think we can put it on life support. I'll need to go into Belle on Monday to get some new parts. Don't fire it up until then. The power company will be here Monday morning to turn on the electricity. Do you want to come with me to Belle? We don't need to be here for them to flip a damn switch."

She smiled. If she could go to the secondhand store, maybe she could find some clothes to wear. "Yes, I could use some jeans and sensible shoes."

Stephanie glanced down at the pair of stiff-soled moccasins she'd worn all day. She'd found them in her mom's closet. They were old but sturdy and much easier to work in than the high-heeled boots she'd worn over to the house that morning.

Well, the bucket wasn't going to empty itself. "Trip one million and one, coming up." Like her mom, she couldn't see pouring dirt down the pipes when she could toss it outside where it came from.

Granted, there would be a small ice-skating pond on the far side of the porch but having the house clean was well worth skirting the area until it melted.

She opened the door and carefully walked over the wooden boards of the wrap-around porch. If she spilled water on the porch, she'd have to salt the boards to keep ice from forming. Salt wasn't a friend of wood. Or so her dad had told her, although she wasn't sure if that was true or not.

A loud groan stopped her, and then a snap dumped her right leg through the porch boards. The bucket spilled over onto her, soaking Declan's sweat-shirt and pants, her t-shirt, and the yoga pants she wore under his sweatpants.

"Damn it!" *You are so stupid.* She'd heard the board groan whenever she took a bucket of water out of the house. Steph shoved the bucket away, and water sloshed out, dousing her again. "Great. Thank you. I really needed that. Like I wasn't cold enough." She braced her hands on the boards and tried to lift herself out of the hole. A sharp pain raced down her leg and flew back up, but the real pain radiated from her ankle.

She groaned and tried again. It was no good. She needed her leg to help her un-wedge from the hole, and she couldn't put any weight on it. So she had one option.

"Declan!" Stephanie screamed his name at the top of her lungs. Thank God it was Saturday, and Moe was opening the bar. "Declaaaaaaaaan!"

The door of Declan's house flung open, and her brother, half-dressed, hair wet, and one boot on, rifle in hand, sprinted across the space between the houses. "What the hell?" He skittered to a stop and blinked at her. "Are you okay?"

"Why the gun?"

"I don't know. Snakes, coyotes, wolves, lynx, wolverines, a psycho skunk?"

She stared up at him, and her mouth dropped open. "Thanks." If he hadn't reminded her of the inherent risks of living in the middle of nowhere, she could have remained blissfully ignorant.

He leaned the rifle against the house. "Do you need me to lift you out of there?"

"Yeah, I think I hurt my ankle." Sprained it, maybe. Probably not broken. She hoped. There had been enough "accidents" in her past to be a pretty good judge of things.

He grabbed her under the armpits and hefted her out of the hole. "Shit." He bent down. "You're cut." He moved the sopping wet sweatpants up her leg, then looked down in the hole. "You got sliced by a nail. When was the last time you had a tetanus shot?"

Stephanie shook her head. "I don't know. I'm not sure." She'd been in and out of various hospitals when Presley was in a rage. Never the same hospital, of course, and she always gave a fake name. Presley would ensure the bill was paid in cash. A handy tool to make sure no questions were asked. Maybe she'd been given a tetanus shot during one of those visits? But she didn't know.

"Hold on." He raced into the house and came out with her cleaning rags.

She tried to stop him. "No, Declan, they're dirty."

"I hate to tell you this, but so are you." He wrapped one around her leg, keeping the sweats and her legging between the dirty material of the cleaning rag, and tied the knot over where the nail had slashed her calf. "Let's go." He picked her and the rifle up, then started down the stairs.

"Where? Where are we going? Stop. You need to turn off the lights and bank the fire."

"Steph, look at that cloth I put around your leg." Declan stopped and waited until she looked down.

"Oh." It had turned dark red in the middle. "Just

take me to the bathroom. I'll clean it up and put a Band-Aid on it."

"No way. You probably need stitches." He put her in the truck.

"No, I don't!" She hated hospitals. Their smell reminded her of the questions she couldn't answer, the lies she repeated, and the brutality she went home to after being examined.

One day, Presley had hurt her, but before he took her to the hospital, he'd choked her until she was unconscious. "Never let yourself be admitted, or you won't wake up," was the last thing she'd heard.

Presley would have killed her if she'd said anything to anyone or asked for help. That was a fact she didn't doubt. Not for a second. He would kill her. He'd promised to do it, and she could see the truth in his eyes. Now, the thought of a hospital sent a chill through her colder than the air freezing her wet clothes.

Declan bolted into his house and emerged less than a minute later, his second boot on but not laced, a t-shirt over his shoulder, and a phone held to his ear. "We're heading in." He tossed the phone onto the seat between them and got into the truck.

Steph was freezing. Fear and the winter elements

converged to make her teeth chatter. "W-who were you talking to?"

"Zeke. He's coming in from the Marshall ranch. We'll get there about the same time."

Zeke. She remembered the attractive doctor. The one she assumed was a vet because of his massive build, but he was actually a medical doctor. She'd seen him once or twice after meeting him at the Bit and Spur. Stephanie dropped her head back against the headrest. He was so handsome and friendly. If she was young enough to have crushes, Zeke was the type of man for which she'd fall head over heels. She shivered harder as the truck's heater blew cold air onto her soaked clothing. As the truck lurched forward and jolted her ankle against the floorboard, she clenched her jaw and closed her eyes. Things had been going so well. She shook her head. That was the story of her life, wasn't it?

3

Zeke hung up the phone and glanced at Adam Cassidy. "Duty calls."

Adam nodded. "No problem. I'll be here until next weekend. Then the wife and I'll be gone for a week. You've got the lay of the land, come out next Friday, and I'll run you through who we have and what's needed. Since we don't have more incoming patients and the ones remaining are transitioning to PT and strengthening programs, most of my work has been the urgent care type. Sniffles and scrapes with a couple of odds and ends thrown in."

Zeke smiled. "That sums up the life of a country doctor. But I wouldn't change it for anything." He loved being a doctor in a rural community. It was the grass-roots medicine he'd always wanted to practice. He glanced at his watch. "I better go."

"One of those urgent care situations?" Adam walked him to the door of the upper-level clinic. Zeke had to sign his life away, promise his hypothetical firstborn child as collateral, and have a security background check completed before he was allowed down into the facility underneath the ranch. Once he saw it, he understood why there were such precautions. Guardian wouldn't let just anyone know about the underground structure.

"Declan's sister fell through an old porch. He thinks she needs stitches and possibly an X-ray." Zeke pulled his keys out of his pocket. He wasn't aware Declan's sister was still around. The woman was striking and beautiful but way too city for him. He preferred a more natural woman. Not that he didn't look at Stephanie. Hell, all the men in Hollister noticed her. Of course, he assumed that was what she wanted. To be noticed. Whatever. She was his patient, so any question of attraction was out the window.

He turned to Adam. "I hope you and the missus have a good vacation."

"We will, although I think our daughter will have more fun. She's staying with Grandma and Grandpa, so she doesn't miss any school. She seems to think she can stay in our house alone while we're gone. Grandpa Frank has other ideas."

Zeke laughed. "I've met Mr. Marshall. I don't think your daughter will win that battle."

"Neither do I." Adam clapped him on the back. "Take care and call out if you need help."

Laughing, Zeke shook his head. "The arrangement was for me to help you."

"Call it a professional courtesy, and let's not forget the fact that I'm getting bored."

"Appreciate it, but, dude, never say things like that. Life can pick up on those words and make you regret them."

Adam smiled. "How right you are. I retract my last statement, but not the offer of help when you need it." Zeke shook the man's hand and then headed out to his truck. He followed the precise route he was told to travel to and from the ranch. He had a gut feeling that if he deviated, he'd be flat on his facc in the middle of the road with high-powered weapons pointed in his direction.

Zeke got it. After the attack on the ranch, the one that they were currently rebuilding from, he understood the reason for the security. He never saw the defenses he assumed were in place, but that was probably by intent rather than chance. To the uninformed eye, the ranch was just that, a functioning ranch. Once you passed the ranch house and went over the hill that separated the Guardian complex from the working ranch, a person's perspective changed.

He made good time to the office. The little town was buttoned up with warm yellow lights drifting out the snow-edged windows. It was a cold January day. There were two vehicles in front of the Bit and Spur. The small bar had its regulars and a steady stream of people wanting an adult beverage. Still, like everywhere else, the intense cold of the South Dakota winters kept people at home, even on Friday and Saturday nights.

Pulling up to the clinic, he got out and jogged up the steps to the back door. It took him a minute to unlock the front of the building, then he popped into his office to boot up his computer and turn the heat up in the exam room. The sound of a vehicle drew him to the front door. He opened it as Declan, sans coat, jogged around the cab of his truck and opened the passenger door.

Zeke moved to help him, but Declan shut the door and was trudging through the snow, carrying his sister, by the time Zeke had made it to the street.

"Bring her in here." Zeke opened the door and directed Declan to the exam room, his eyes glued to the filthy, bloody rag tied around the woman's calf.

"Let's get this out of the way." He grabbed a scissor, cut through the wet material, moved the soaked sweatpants, found another layer of leggings, and lifted them away from the open wound. He glanced up at Declan's sister and did a double-take. Her blonde hair, usually perfectly straight, was a halo of curls that fell to her shoulders from the remainder of what once might have been a bun on the top of her head. She wore no makeup. Hell, if he'd seen her on the street, he wouldn't have recognized her. To stay on track, he batted away the thought. "Tell me what happened."

"I was taking the last bucket of mop water out of the old place. A board on the porch gave away, and I fell through it. The bucket dumped on me, and somewhere in that moment, I twisted my ankle."

"The cut was from an old nail under the porch," Declan added as Stephanie shivered.

Zeke nodded. "Okay, we need to get you out of these wet clothes. Declan, go to my office. In the closet, there are a couple of clean pairs of scrubs. Grab a set, would you?"

"On it." The man scooted out of the room.

While he was gone, Zeke did the intake. The standard questions and information that every medical practitioner required. The ubiquitous, do you have any known allergies, plus a quick scan for a temp and the blood pressure cuff on her arm. He also asked about her weight. Standing on a scale with one good foot while sopping wet and bleeding wasn't a priority.

"This cut isn't too deep, but it'll probably leave a scar." Zeke went to work on the wound as quickly as he could before he tended to her swollen ankle. "You said you were cleaning?" he asked to keep her talking and distract her from how cold she must be.

"Yeah. Can't stay with D-Declan any longer." She wrapped her arms around herself. He glanced up. She was pale, her lips drawn tight. She was in pain, but she wasn't complaining about it.

"No room?" Zeke asked in a distracted way that put his patients at ease. He was a master of keeping his patients talking while he worked.

"No, she doesn't like my overnight guests," Declan said as he returned with a pair of dark green scrubs.

Zeke looked up from his task to take in the cat devouring the cream smile on Declan's face. Zeke shook his head. "My mom didn't raise a fool. I'm not even going to ask."

"No need to ask. I'll tell you. His overnight guests are noisy," Steph said and huffed a soft laugh.

"What can I say?" Declan spread his arms out. "Women like me."

"All night long," Steph added, and both laughed, which put a smile on Zeke's face. He kind of liked disheveled Stephanie. He'd met her a time or two and was impressed with her clothes and all the fancy makeup, but she'd seemed distant and reserved, almost ... manufactured. Maybe manufactured wasn't the right word, but she wasn't really herself. Hell, that didn't make sense, did it? He hadn't seen her in months and assumed she'd left town.

Zeke finished cleaning the wound and looked up. "Okay. Give me a minute to get this wound closed up with butterfly bandages, and I'll wrap it to protect it. I don't think you need stitches. I'm going to give you some antibiotics as a precaution. When was your last tetanus shot?"

"I c-couldn't say for sure." Stephanie shivered as she spoke, shifting and putting her arms back onto the table where she sat.

A loud squelch of suction, which sounded like a tremendous fart, echoed in the room.

Her hand flew to her mouth, and she squeaked, "Oh my God." Stephanie's eyes grew wide. "It was my clothes. They were stuck to the table."

"Sure, they were." Declan's belly laugh earned him a slap with a wet sleeve.

Zeke hid his smile. He could imagine the woman was mortified. Clothes or the relief of gas, it didn't matter. The situation was crudely funny. He finished dressing the injury, but Declan was still taunting his sister, and to her credit, she took it like a champ.

"We'll get out of here and let you change. Don't put any pressure on your ankle. If you stand, make sure you're within reach of the table so you can balance yourself. Do you need help?" He nodded toward the soaked gray sweatshirt and pants.

She shook her head and pulled her hands through the tangle of curls that destroyed the last of the bun at the top of her head. She looked so tiny in Declan's oversized sweats. "No, thank you. I'll be okay."

"Hold on a second." Zeke ducked out of the exam room and grabbed a large garbage bag for her to put her wet clothes in and a towel, so she could dry off. "For your clothes and for you. We'll be right outside if you need us." Zeke motioned to Declan.

"You can let it rip now, Steph." Declan laughed as he left the room.

"Just get out." Steph groaned.

"Man, did you see how red her face got?" Declan asked, still chuckling.

"It was rather embarrassing." Zeke leaned against the wall.

"She used to be fun all the time. The gossips around here hardened her." Declan's happy demeanor shifted. "She left with the intent of never coming back."

"She's back now."

"Yeah." Declan nodded. "She's a good person, doc."

He frowned at the man who'd moved from acquaintance to friend over the years. That friendship was solidified when he'd treated Declan for a knife wound he sustained outside his bar. "Dude, why would you think I assume she's not?"

"Rumors. Vicious gossip," Declan spat the words out.

"I don't listen to rumors. I don't have the time or the mental bandwidth to keep up with it. Well, except for when Edna was tracking UFOs."

"Man, she sure was tripping out. Edna is an okay lady. Nosey, sure, but Donna Franks was the one stirring up shit against Stephanie. That woman had it out for her."

Zeke cocked his head. "I don't know a Donna Franks."

"She moved before you came to town. After she ran Steph off, she went to live with her daughter in Nebraska."

Zeke nodded. He wasn't into gossip, not even gossip about gossips.

Declan continued, "Just wanted you to know, my sister is a decent person. She's been through a lot."

Zeke lifted his eyes to look at his friend. "I make my own assessments and judgments about people. I assure you of that."

Declan nodded. "That's all she needs, a fair shake."

"She'll get it from me." And why was it so significant to Declan that Zeke had an open mind about his sister? Whatever the reason, it seemed important to his friend. He could tell that much.

Zeke changed the subject. "Hey, are you still looking for someone to help on Friday and Saturday nights?"

Declan nodded. "Yeah, need someone to keep up with the washing and such. Why? Do you have a candidate?"

"Maybe. Young kid, maybe eighteen or so. Family is down on their luck."

"Perfect. The kid won't handle alcohol, so he doesn't have to be twenty-one. What's his name?"

"Clay Thompson. Might be a week or so before he shows up."

"That would work for me," Declan said, leaning against the wall. "We're slow now, but when the weather breaks, people will show up."

"All right, I'm decent," Stephanie called out from the other side of the door.

Zeke opened the door and chuckled. His scrubs were giant on her, but she'd rolled the pants up and cinched the drawstring, pinning the hugely oversized top to her tiny waist. Her hair fell to her shoulders in ringlets. She stood with her leg bent at the knee, elevating her ankle. "They're gi-normous." Holding the shoulder, she pulled the fabric out. Four or five women her size could have fit in the shirt. "I didn't want to get back on." She pointed to the white paper that had dissolved under her wet, dirty clothes.

"I can fix that." Zeke cleaned the exam table and placed a fresh paper sheet over the plastic cover.

Declan's cell phone ringing caught his attention, and he answered. "Yeah, sure. Hold on." Declan covered the speaker of his phone. “Zeke, Moe is feeling like crap. Thinks he has the flu. He tried to gut it out. Curly convinced him he needed to go home before he left.”

“I can come back,” Stephanie offered.

Zeke shook his head. “Get Moses home. I don’t need anyone else spreading that damn flu around. I can take Stephanie out to your place when we’re done.”

“Thanks.” Declan turned to leave.

“Wipe down everything he touched with a disinfectant,” Zeke called after him.

“Planning on it,” Declan called back.

“You don’t have to take me home. I can call someone.” Stephanie blinked up at him. Without her makeup and that ... well, for lack of a better word, the attitude she usually carried around like a sword, she looked younger and more vulnerable. Cute even. He put the brakes on that line of thinking. *Thou shalt not think those things of thy patient.* No matter how good they looked.

He shrugged. “I’m here. No sense in bringing someone out in the cold. Let’s look at that ankle.” He helped her back onto the table and carefully examined the joint. The swelling and bruising had doubled the ankle’s size. It looked like soft tissue damage, but he needed to make sure.

“Okay, let me get a chair to take you into the X-ray room.”

“Wait, how far is it? Can’t I just hop?” Her eyes darted around the room in a panic.

“Afraid of wheelchairs?” He folded his arms across his chest and stared at the woman.

“What? No, it's just that I’m not hurt that bad. It isn’t broken. I can tell.” She gave a nervous laugh. “Wheelchairs mean you're admitted. I don’t want that. It was just a stupid accident. For real.”

He cocked his head and repeated her words, “For real?”

She shot him a frightened look. “It’s just a saying. I’ll hop.”

“I’d rather you didn’t.”

“I’m going to hop,” Stephanie said as she slid off the exam table and away from him. “Which way?”

A tingle of “that’s weird” hit him. He pointed to the next room and watched as she hopped one step toward the door. He shook his head, seeing disaster in the making as the scrub pants unrolled and pooled around her good foot.

He moved behind her, ready to catch her when she fell. “You’re going to slip.”

"What?" She turned around, and her hand missed the door jamb she grabbed to steady herself. Zeke swooped in and lifted her into his arms. She was smaller and lighter than he'd assumed, but she was also tense as a cat in a room full of hungry dogs.

"Sorry, I'm sorry." Her face was flushed when he sat her down.

"Stubborn much?" He laughed when she groaned.

She shivered again. "I'm sorry. I just don't like hospitals."

Zeke pointed to the ceiling and circled his finger. "You mentioned that before, but this is a clinic. Not a hospital. No need to stress out about being here."

Stephanie lifted her eyes and nodded but didn't comment. Zeke took that as his cue to get started. He took several shots of the ankle and left her where she was to look at the X-rays. He wasn't going to risk her nose-planting in the hallway with the hopping routine again.

After he reviewed the pictures, he stopped by the supply closet and retrieved three compression bandages. "Good news. No broken bones."

"Okay. Good. Rest, ice, compression, and elevation." Stephanie listed off the exact protocol for a sprain.

"Have a lot of sprains?"

Her smile was more like a grimace. "Sprains, strains, other things." He sensed she was watching him carefully as he wrapped her ankle. "Thank you for catching me out there."

He glanced up at her, and her eyes darted away. "You're welcome. Besides, what kind of person would I be if I didn't help?"

She shrugged. "Some don't."

He finished bandaging her ankle and gave her the extra wraps. "I'm not that person, and I'd stay far away from those who would let you fall."

"Sage advice. Thanks for these," she said, lifting the rolled compression bandages.

"I'll get the tetanus shot ready and pull your antibiotics." He administered the shot and gave her the antibiotics he had in stock in the drug cabinet. They kept everything under lock and key but maintained a healthy stock of drugs due to the remoteness of their location. He took off his latex gloves and tossed them in the waste bin before saying, "Now, we get to do the dirty work."

Her head snapped in his direction. "What?"

He laughed at her shocked expression and lifted both hands. "Paperwork. Do you have insurance?"

She shook her head. "I'll pay in cash. I can do that, right?"

Zeke nodded. "Sure. Can I get you that wheelchair or loan you a set of crutches?"

She glanced up at him. "Crutches, please."

"Give me a second." He grabbed a pair of aluminum crutches someone had donated to the clinic and adjusted them for her height. She used them like a champ, and he directed her to his office. He hated the paperwork part of his job. The receptionist slash bookkeeper the county had funded was a full-time position. Still, the pay was less than people could make working part-time. Since Guardian employed both him and Jeremiah, the company had offered to subsidize the state's pay to help them out. They needed to get that paperwork done, so he didn't have to continue doing the billing. Granted, it went into the system, and the accountants down in Belle Fourche sent the bills, but still, it wasn't what he went to medical school to do.

"Are you using Declan's address?" He pulled up the sheets he needed to complete.

"Yes. The old place has the same address. The bill will get to me." Stephanie pushed her hair back and out of her face.

He groaned when the field grayed out and hit the

backspace, muttering under his breath. The program was a pain in the ass to work. She leaned forward, "What are you doing?"

He tilted the screen toward her. "Entering your information. This portion of the job is the bane of my medical existence. I can dictate my notes, but the billing part of the profession is tedious."

"I worked as a data specialist at an insurance agency in Denver for a couple of years. I liked it."

Zeke keyed into that bit of information like a stray dog tracking a T-bone steak. "Do you have a job?"

STEPH FLINCHED at the sharp question. What had she said? Why did Zeke snap at her? What did she do? Her life with Presley had conditioned her to react, flinch, and try to avoid being hit. God, she needed to stop being so afraid. She tried to straighten her shoulders before she asked, "Is that required to fill out the forms?"

Zeke looked confused and concerned at her reaction, but thankfully, he didn't ask. He shook his head. "No, sorry, I didn't mean to scare you just now. We're searching for someone to be a receptionist and do the billing for myself and Doctor Wheeler. The position is still being finalized as well as the pay, but if you have experience ..."

Relief and a sense of hope washed over her. She smiled and shook her head. "I don't have a job and *am* looking for one." A job at a doctor's office would be perfect. She could wear the clothes she'd brought with her until she had enough money to buy a more appropriate wardrobe. "I worked mainly with claims management software, but I also worked with analytic software. It detected if the claimants were making fraudulent claims. I'm fairly familiar with the medical claims system as that was where the majority of the fraudulent claims came."

As Zeke leaned back in his chair, Steph couldn't help but notice the bulk of his arms and shoulders and how his shirt molded to the plates of muscle in his chest. No wonder he could pick her up as if she weighed nothing. The feel of his arms around her had initially terrified her. Still, there was care in his mannerisms, something she'd never felt around Presley. Except for Declan, she didn't let any man near her anymore. Which was why she didn't want to work at the bar. Life with Presley haunted her, but she couldn't let anyone know. It was why she put on an act and flaunted the personality the town expected her to have. She flirted to keep the illusion, but God, it had killed her. That was why she'd stopped coming into town. At a doctor's office, she'd have to be professional. That would explain her personality change. It wasn't like she'd be doing anything except coming in to work.

Shit.

She didn't have a car to use. The Mercedes was the one link to Presley; if anyone asked about the damn thing ... She pulled her bottom lip into her mouth. She could look around for a used truck.

"I can see the wheels turning," Zeke spoke to her, and she snapped her attention back to him. His blue eyes sparkled at her, and his smile was friendly and open. "What has you thinking so hard?"

She smiled back at him. "I don't have a way to get to work."

"Well, that could be an issue, but let's open the position and do an official interview before we worry about transportation."

The heat of embarrassment ran to her cheeks. Of course, she didn't have the job. Presley would have mocked her and probably cuffed her a good one for assuming. God, she'd never learn, would she? She was as stupid as Presley had repeatedly told her, wasn't she? "Right. Sorry." She nodded to the phone.

"If you don't mind, I'll call Declan and tell him I'll stay with him until closing."

"Hey, what just happened there? I do need to interview candidates." Zeke leaned forward, and instinctively, she jerked back out of his reach. Not that he was reaching for her. Shit. Her gut tightened, and she couldn't breathe.

"I understand that. I was being stupid. I'm sorry."

Zeke cocked his head, and he stared at her. "I don't think you were being stupid. Excited, maybe, but definitely not stupid."

She nodded and tried to smile at him, but in her mind, she was in front of Presley. The feelings welling up inside her had nothing to do with what Zeke said but what had happened to her when she'd said or done something stupid, which was all the time. She clenched her hands to stop them from shaking. Damn it, she wished she could control those attacks, but after leaving, they reared their head when they wanted. She cleared her throat and clenched her hands together to keep them from shaking. "May I use your phone?"

"Sure. I'll give you some privacy." He locked his computer screen, stood up, and stared at her again but left the office, closing the door behind himself.

"Bit and Spur." Declan answered the phone on the second ring.

"Declan, could I stay with you at the bar until closing?"

"Yeah, sure. It's dead as a doornail here. I'll probably close early anyway. I thought Zeke was going to take you home?"

"Change of plans."

"Whatever. Do you need me to come to get you? Like I said, there isn't anyone here."

"Please."

"Be right there."

She hung up the phone and wiped a tear that spilled down her cheek. A loser. She was such a loser. The doctor had been logical. She'd jumped at the chance and didn't temper her response. Lord, how embarrassing. Zeke must think she was mental. Maybe she was.

ZEKE CLOSED the supply closet and leaned against the door. What had happened in there? Stephanie had more going on than a strained ankle, and that was concerning. His interest was piqued by the woman he'd met tonight. The one who laughed with her brother, blushed in embarrassment at fart noises, and was stubborn enough not to want to ride in a wheelchair. She was cute, and until she crawled into her shell in the office, she'd been engaging.

He rubbed his neck and leaned against the wall as he listened to the slight sound of her voice as she talked on the phone. He had no idea what he did or said that caused her to pull away, physically or mentally. A shame, really. That version of Stephanie Howard was one he'd like to get to know.

4

The drive to Belle Fourche took about an hour and a half, and Zeke used the time to call his mom and check in with her and Pete. He tried to call about once a week, but that varied depending on how busy he was.

"Hello, who is this?"

He laughed, "It hasn't been that long, Mom."

"Oh, sure, you know, I was just saying to Pete that our boy had to be abducted by aliens or something."

Zeke laughed harder. He'd filled his mom in on Edna's UFO search. "Someone broke it to her that she was wasting her time."

"Why? You told me she was happy digging for information." His mom had met Edna once or twice when she and Pete had come to Hollister to visit.

"She was, but all good things must come to an end."

"Well, she had a mission for a while. Good for her." She clicked her tongue. "I saw Felicia at the grocery store. She said to say hi."

"How is Felicia?" His high school girlfriend was a sweet girl who'd married sometime after he'd left for college. She and her husband had moved several times before settling in Florida, in the same town as his parents. His mom had literally bumped into her with her shopping cart about five years ago.

"She's finally pregnant. I told you they've been doing that in vitro thing, right? Well, it took." His mother sighed. "She looked exhausted but good."

"She's happy, though?"

"Yeah, she glows when she talks about her pregnancy and Keith. His air conditioning business is doing well, too." His mom filled him in and then changed the topic. "When can we expect you for a visit? You missed Thanksgiving and Christmas. What about Easter?"

"I might be able to swing that. Depends on whether or not Eden can cover for me." And if Guardian needed him during that time, but his mother didn't need to know about that.

"Well, we'd love to see you. Pete has that old boat all fixed up and wants to show it off."

"I still have things to do to it," Pete said in the background.

His mom snorted, "Oh, you'll be fussing with that silly thing forever."

"That's why I bought it." Pete laughed, and Zeke could see the man's smile in his mind. Pete was a great man and treated his mom the way she deserved to be treated.

"What's the weather like in Florida on this beautiful January day?" Zeke reached over and turned up the heater of his truck. The thermostat on the dashboard read negative five degrees.

"Oh, sixties today. We have the windows open, but the neighbors are bundled up." His mom laughed. "Sooner or later, our South Dakota blood will defrost, and we'll be cold at this temperature, too."

"You've been in Florida for almost fifteen years, Mom. If you were going to thaw, it would have happened."

"True. How's life up there?" Which was code for, "Are you dating?"

"Busy. Work has shifted from outdoor type

injuries for the most part." Stephanie falling through the porch the day before yesterday aside. "Flu, colds, and the usual stuff."

There was silence before his mom asked. "Met anyone new?"

He sighed. "Nope, but I'm fine, Mom."

"I know, I know, it's just that I worry about you being alone."

"I'm not alone. I have a town full of friends and you and Pete." Zeke pulled up over the hill, and he sighed at the sight of Belle Fourche.

"It's not the same."

He sighed again. "Mom, we're not doing this again."

"Okay, okay. So, what are you doing today?" Thankfully, she'd let it go.

"I'm driving into Belle. I need to pick up a few things for a family down on their luck. Eden has call. What do you have planned?"

"Oh, you're such a caring man. I swear you have a wonderful heart. I don't know why some woman hasn't tackled and hog-tied you."

"Mom." He groaned the word.

"Fine, fine. Let's see, what are we doing, right? Well, I'm going to the movies with Iris, and Bill and Pete are going to watch the playoffs." His mom laughed. "Even though his team didn't make it in."

"Doesn't matter. It's football." He heard Pete say essentially the same thing at about the same time. He laughed at his mom's groan. Zeke actually had his DVR set to record. One of the very few things he loved to watch. Thank goodness Sunday afternoon and Mondays were his "off" days. If he had to make a trip to the south on Sunday, he turned off his radio, so he wouldn't know the scores, so he could watch the games he recorded on Monday. He'd played in college and was pretty good as a tight end, but his calling was medicine. It always had been.

"Oh, there's Iris and Bill," his mom said right before the doorbell rang, and his mom's peek-a-poo went into a rapid-fire, high-pitched yipping tirade.

"I'll let you go, then. Love you, Mom."

"Tilly, hush. I love you, too. Be safe. Tilly!" His mom hushed the dog again. It worked just as well as it did the first time. As in, it didn't.

"Always." He disconnected and shook his head. His mom was nothing if not persistent.

Belle Fourche wasn't huge, but it had a western clothier with good clothes, a boot repair shop, and warm coats. He pulled into the parking lot and made his way inside. He dropped off his boots for repair and rambled around the store for a few minutes before he selected three coats and put them on the counter. "Could you hold these for me? I want to do some more shopping."

"Sure." The woman behind the counter took the coats and hung them behind the counter. He headed to the jeans and pulled six pairs of what he thought were the suitable sizes out of the stacks. It would be better if they were too big than too little. He placed them on the counter, and the woman gave him a quizzical look when he said he'd be back.

Zeke went to the far end of the store and picked out three pairs of lace-up boots. Again, a guess, but he erred on larger rather than smaller. He placed the boots on the counter, and the woman's eyebrows raised, but he gave her credit; she didn't ask. "Just a few more things." He turned and went back to the jeans, where he selected a couple of pairs and then headed to the changing booth. He'd put on bulk in his thighs from weightlifting and needed a couple of pairs of jeans that weren't skintight.

He toggled on the light switch to the changing room, but it didn't come on. Whatever. He went in to change. Thank God he'd picked up the second pair in a bigger size and relaxed fit.

"I don't need new clothes, Declan. I can get by with stuff from the secondhand store."

Zeke straightened. He recognized that voice.

Declan growled, "Stop, Steph. I can afford to buy you some shirts, jeans, and decent shoes. Just get in and try them on. I'll be right back. Give me your crutches, and I'll prop them out here."

Zeke chuckled to himself and sat down to put his boots on, listening to Stephanie grumble. Still, he heard material flapping, so she was letting her brother take care of her.

"Hey, Steph, try this on—what the fuck happened to your back?"

"Crap, Declan, can you knock?" Stephanie shrieked.

"Are those cigarette burns?" Declan's voice was incredulous.

"Stop, let me go!" Stephanie ground out the words. "Just get out."

Declan sounded sick when he asked, "He fucking burned you?"

Stephanie hissed, "I'm not discussing this here, and stop yelling."

Zeke heard Declan lower his voice. "There's no one here but us. What the hell happened?"

There was silence for a moment, then

Stephanie's voice, "He wasn't a good man. I'll explain, but not here. Please, Declan, not now."

Zeke dropped his head back. Dear God, cigarette burns on her back. What kind of fucking animal did that?

"We'll take these. Get your shirt and clothes on. We have a lot of talking to do," Declan snapped. "Shit. I'm sorry. Steph. You don't have to flinch away from me. I'd never hit you. I'm not mad at you. I'm mad at that bastard who put those burns on your back."

He could hear Stephanie sniffle. "I know. I do. I just can't help it."

Zeke's thoughts flashed back to how she'd jumped when he'd asked if she had a job. Fuck, he hadn't startled her. He'd *scared* her. Steph had been in an abusive relationship. That explained so many of the comments he'd written off. Fuck.

He heard the door shut, Stephanie moving around, and then the door open. Declan's voice was much softer, kinder as if he'd purposefully taken the time to control his outrage. "Come on. I'll buy us some lunch. I'm sorry I snapped at you." Damn good on him. There was no way in hell Zeke would be able to do that. Not for a hot minute, that was for sure. When he'd done his rotation at medical school, an abused woman came into the emergency room one night. She'd claimed she'd fallen, but the bruises and contusions told a different story. Zeke had called the cops, but by the time they'd arrived, the woman had checked herself out against medical advice. Three days later, the man she went back to cracked her skull. She died in the same emergency room. The anger of that incident never went away. He followed the court case. At least that bastard was convicted for his crime and couldn't abuse any other women. God, the words he'd overheard explained so much. The manufactured personality that didn't show the real person. How in the hell had she survived? The woman he'd heard just then had every right to wear her armor, but he'd give anything to help her lose the shield and realize she didn't have to live in fear.

Zeke slowly counted to two hundred, then opened the changing room door. Declan and Stephanie were at the counter, so he took his time, grabbed two more pairs of jeans in the size he needed, and stayed out of their line of sight. When they left, he made his way to the counter. "All done?"

"Yes, thank you. Would you put those jeans in a separate bag and take the price tags off everything else?"

"Sure." The woman shrugged off the request and started checking him out. He paid for his purchases and toted the bags out to the truck. As he sat in the driver's seat, he stared out the window at the gray clouds billowing over the small town. It would snow again. He glanced at his watch. He'd grab the groceries he needed and head back north.

Two and a half hours later, he pulled into a small turnout off the highway, trundling down a pot-hole-infested trail some would call a road. He wouldn't. He drove slowly to the end and put the vehicle in park. The small fifth-wheel camper was leveled as best as possible on the semi-flat patch of ground. He got out, lifted the bags containing the clothes and boots, and took them to the door.

The door opened, and a thin boy, about eighteen, stepped out. He was wearing a threadbare sweater and old tennis shoes. "Doc, what are you doing here?"

"Hey, Clay. Brought you some stuff."

The boy looked back at the trailer. "They'll be upset. They don't take charity."

"They can deal with it. I'm not giving you charity. I'm being neighborly." Zeke handed the boy the bags. "I'll be right back." He jogged back to the truck and hefted three large bags out of the back. "Where are your dad and gramps?"

"Gramps is sleeping. Dad walked that way. He saw some antelope tracks." Clay Thompson shook his head. "We've had a string of bad luck. The meat would be good."

"Poaching is frowned on around here. Don't let the game warden or the deputy sheriff catch any of you hunting without a license."

"Wouldn't do it if we weren't in this position." Clay said. "We aren't criminals. Just hungry and needing a break."

Zeke could see it was true. When he was in the camper, it was neat as a pin, there were no indications of drugs or alcohol, and all three of the men were respectful and polite. "Figured. Is your grandpa's hand and arm better?"

"Yeah. Seems to be healing well. We're watching for the signs you said to look for. Why are you doing this for us?" Clay looked at him. "We got nothing to pay you back."

"I'm doing this because I can. Someday, when you can help out people in need, I hope you'll do the same."

"Seems like we've been on this end of the help for a long time. If I ever get to your end of the stick,

I'd be honored to help out." Clay shifted from side to side. "Someday, I'll make it."

Zeke didn't doubt it. The family needed a break. Maybe his assistance would be the thing that tipped the scales in their favor. "I believe you." Zeke put the bags on the step and reached into his wallet. Clay held up his hand. "No, sir. I can't take any cash."

Zeke pulled out five hundred dollars that he'd withdrawn from the ATM in Belle Fourche. "This is to get your truck fixed and gas and some more propane. You'll be freezing soon if you don't restock that propane tank. There's work around the area, but you'll need transportation to get to the ranches to find it. I talked to my friend Declan; he's looking for a bar back. You don't have to be twenty-one, just be willing to clean tables and glasses and take out the trash on Friday and Saturday nights. You won't be touching the alcohol. He's out at the Bit and Spur, just outside of town. He'll be looking for you to show up when the truck is fixed. Your dad can head out to the Hollisters' place. Heard they may be taking on a hand or two."

Clay shivered. "Dad will be sorry he missed you. But, like I said, he's prideful about taking charity."

There was a chance Zeke would hurt the man's pride but taking care of his family should be Mitch's,

Clay's father's, primary focus, not on the unknown benefactor of a few basic necessities. "He'll make the right choice. Take this inside, cook a good meal for all three of you, and have your dad get Phil from the garage to tow the truck into Hollister and get it fixed."

"I'll do my best." Clay took the cash and shoved it into his back pocket. He accepted the bags and struggled a bit under the weight. "Thank you, Doc. Thank you so much. You really don't know how much this will help."

He did. He knew all too well. He'd seen folks on hard times. He had enough to share with those who'd been taken to the mat. And Clay's family had been laid flat. He'd talked with the men when he stitched up Clay's grandpa. They were trying to fix the truck by themselves without proper tools, and one of the wrenches had slipped from where it was leveraged and punctured the palm of old Chester's hand. Clay had walked to town to fetch the doctor. That was how he'd come to find the family parked on what he believed to be Hollister land. Zeke refused to take payment for the work, brushing it off as nothing but a neighborly act.

"Take care of them, Clay." He winked at the boy.

"I do try, sir. They're pretty stubborn."

"I can see that." Zeke lifted his hand and headed to his truck and back into Hollister. Once he got back onto the highway, he called Phil. If the bill was over three hundred dollars, he'd pay it. No need for the Thompsons to know.

5

Stephanie didn't pay much attention to where Declan was taking her until he'd parked, and she looked up to see they'd arrived at a little diner on Fifth Avenue. They were in front of a family-run business that served breakfast all day, but she wasn't going to eat. Her stomach was tied in knots. Why hadn't she locked the dressing room door? Why hadn't Declan knocked?

She watched him shut off the engine before she asked, "Why didn't you knock?"

"I was gone like ten seconds." He scrubbed his face. "I need to know what happened, Steph. My mind has been racing with all types of nightmarish shit."

She chuffed a breath of air and shook her head. "It was a nightmare. You read the news articles about women who find themselves isolated and alone, with no hope of removing themselves from the situation. You think, man, that stuff could never happen to me." She stared at a couple who darted into the diner, getting out of the cold. "I didn't see it, and by the time I did, I was so scared." She twirled her finger in her hair, which she'd straightened for the first time in months. "He was so sweet at the beginning."

Declan sighed. "What's his name?"

She snapped her gaze to him. "No. You'll do something stupid."

Declan growled a bit and dropped his head back against the headrest. "You could report him for domestic abuse. Testify against him and get him thrown in jail."

She stared at him a moment. "Don't you think I thought of that? He's untouchable." She'd accompanied him to police benefit dinners and private events with the district attorney and mayor. No one would believe her.

"No one's untouchable." Declan's jaw bulged as he ground his teeth together.

"He is. I'm out of the situation, Declan. The only connection I have to him is that car." She'd love to take a sledgehammer to it and make it unrecognizable.

They were quiet for a moment as Stephanie thought of ways to get rid of that car. Nothing viable came to mind, though. TNT wasn't an option, unfortunately.

"What did he do to you?"

She slowly looked at her brother. "Do you want details? Really?"

Declan ran his hands through his thick mop of blond hair. "Shit. No, and yes. Fuck, Steph, why didn't you call me?"

She smiled at her older brother. "Because of this. This anger you have and the need to be my knight in shining armor. I love you, but this wasn't your war to fight. It still isn't."

"When are you going to stand up for yourself, Steph?"

A dousing of ice water would have been less of a shock. "What?"

"You let them run you out of town instead of calling bullshit. You let this guy hurt you."

What? "That's what you think of me? That I *let*

this guy hurt me? I didn't *let* him hit me in the face so hard I lost two teeth. I didn't *let* him hold me down and burn my back with a lit cigarette! I didn't *let* him do a damn thing, Declan. He was vicious, and I was in fear for my life! I wanted to live and did anything I could to ensure I did. You have no idea what I went through. None!"

"No, I don't because you aren't telling me shit."

A knock on Declan's window made him spin away. He rolled down the window, and a police officer stood with his arms crossed, staring at Declan before sweeping his gaze to Stephanie. "Is there a problem here?"

"No," they said in unison.

"Right. Can I see some identification, please?"

"We were just having a heated discussion," Declan explained as he fished out his wallet.

"Your 'discussion' could be heard inside my vehicle without the window rolled down." The cop nodded to the patrol vehicle parked a foot away. Stephanie hadn't even realized someone had pulled up next to them.

Declan handed the man his driver's license. "Sorry, just some family issues."

"May I see your identification, miss?"

Stephanie jolted. "Sure. Sorry." She dug into her purse and produced the Colorado driver's license she'd been issued when she moved there.

"This is expired." The patrolman glanced back at her.

"Yep. That's why I'm not driving, and he is." She pointed at Declan.

"Mrs. Howard, would you mind stepping out of the truck?" the patrolman requested.

Shit. Her ankle. Thank God Declan had stowed the crutches behind the seat. The officer couldn't see them. "It's miss. I'm his sister." Stephanie said. "I'm not in any trouble, officer. We were arguing, and I'm sorry if we got loud, but I'm perfectly fine." She knew the words to say. She'd said them before at hospitals and a couple of times when Presley had gotten out of hand in public locations. "Honestly, I'd hop out of this truck in a heartbeat if I weren't. He's overprotective and growly, but he's not abusive."

The officer stared at her for a long minute. "I'll be right back."

"What's he going to do?" Stephanie asked as the officer walked back to his patrol car.

"Run us to see if any warrants are outstanding, I'd guess."

Stephanie felt her heart drop to her knees. "The car?"

Declan looked at her. "If he reported that you stole it, you're screwed."

"Shit." She grabbed her brother's arm. "You know nothing about anything. Promise me."

"Steph," he growled her name.

She knew what that meant. He would play protector. "Damn it, Declan, this is me taking control of my life. Don't tell me to stand up for myself and not allow me to do it," she hissed the words at him.

The officer got out of his car and came back to the window. "All right. I recommend finding a more private location to have your family arguments."

"Thank you, officer. We will." Declan handed her driver's license back to her and dropped his into his cup holder.

"Have a good day." The officer walked toward the front door of the diner.

Stephanie waited until he was inside the diner before whispering, "Let's go. Please."

Declan started the truck. "Not a bad idea." He put the truck in gear and headed north.

"I didn't let them run me out of town. I wanted to go, and it was an excuse," she said as they cleared the outskirts of the town. "Donna Franks was wicked, but I could have fought back. I didn't cheat on Andrew. We talked when Andrew came back from college. Neither of us wanted to get married. It was best we went our separate ways. He let me go, and I ran. I ran so fucking fast." She shook her head. "I took the chicken's way out."

Declan nodded. "I hated it for you. I still do. Hated Andrew for a long time, too."

"None of what happened was on Andrew. You have to know that." She shook her head. "He was in a no-win situation, just like I was. His father is such an overbearing tyrant." Senior Hollister was well known for his curt nature, and people in Hollister had seen Andrew take the brunt of the man's wrath most of his life.

Declan snorted. "He's mellowed, it seems."

"Really? Huh, good for Andrew and Gen. She seems nice, by the way," Stephanie said almost as an afterthought because Gen did seem nice and a good match for Andrew, too.

"You can start fresh, you know. You don't have to hide at my house."

"Hide? Yeah, maybe I have been doing that a bit, but mostly, I've been doing a lot of soul-searching and working through what happened in Colorado. If

Zeke actually posts that job I told you about, I'll apply for it. My money is dwindling."

"I still have Dad's truck. It runs and is reliable enough to drive back and forth to town. That way, the car can stay where it is."

She turned in her seat, "Really? I swear I'll pay you back for anything it costs you."

Declan glanced her way, his brows pulled together in irritation. "No, you won't. I'm not poor, Steph. The bar does good business. Moe is currently my only employee. I can afford to buy you clothes and fix the furnace and the truck. There's nothing to worry about."

"Okay." She nodded. "Thank you. I don't want to be a financial burden to you."

"Right, you eat like a bird, keep my house clean, and give me money I don't need for groceries you don't eat. But that's not what I meant, Steph. I mean, there's nothing to worry about. Think about it. There isn't anything in the legal system about the car. He hasn't reported it or you. If there were something in the system, that cop in Belle would have arrested you. You don't have to worry about that guy from Colorado looking for you. You can breathe easy."

She blinked at her brother, then turned her gaze to the road in front of them. She let his words sink in. Free. Was she really free? A specter of doubt perched itself on her shoulder and whispered words that already resided in her soul. *He'll find you.* The law might not be a problem, but Presley most definitely was. She'd probably never stop looking over her shoulder.

6

Zeke pulled into the Kinzers' dairy. The sun wouldn't wake up for at least another two hours. Still, the dairy lights flooded the area in a yellow hue of artificial illumination. As he got out of his truck and pulled out his medical duffle, he heard a call, "Doc, over here."

He shut his truck door and trudged through the snow and dirt to the milking barn. "How's he doing?"

"Hurting. That damn cow caught Dougie on the jaw. I think it's busted, Doc. Dad's worried, too, so you know it isn't good." Elaine Kinzer opened the door to the dairy, where half the herd was in milking stations with their cups attached. "Doug, the doc's here."

Zeke kneeled beside his patient. “Doug, why are you letting cows kick you?”

The man lifted his head, and Zeke’s eyes narrowed. “Yeah, don’t try to answer that.”

Doug’s mandible was broken or, at the bare minimum, dislocated. Zeke’s bet was broken. The gap between the upper and lower was too extreme to be just a dislocation. “Elaine, call the ambulance and tell them to alert Rapid we have a possible broken mandible that may require surgery.”

“That kick rail sure as hell didn’t do its job.” Charlie, Elaine and Doug’s father, stepped up behind him as he spoke.

“No, sir, it didn’t. But Doug will be just fine. We’ll get him patched up.” Zeke kept his voice confident.

Charlie swallowed hard and spoke in a rough voice. “I got the insurance. I want him treated good.”

“He’d be treated well whether or not he had insurance, Charlie.” Zeke made a note to tell the intake personnel he was covered, though.

“Know it, just want him better. Should have redone these kick rails. Moved them up some.”

“We’re at the recommended level required by OSHA.” Dana, Doug’s mom, said from beside her husband. “That cow’s just a bitch.”

“Language,” Charlie said in a distracted type of

way. His wife made a face but didn't say anything else.

Elaine came back and said, "I called. They're on their way. Are you doing this to get out of chores, Dougie?" Elaine dropped down and stared at her brother. "Hell of a way. You could have said you had diarrhea or something."

Doug made a laughing sound, then moaned. Elaine pulled away and winced. "Damn. Sorry."

"Language." Charlie chastised his daughter. "Them cows are about ready to come off the cups. I'll be there in a minute."

"Take care of my boy, Doc. These two are our world." Doug's mom gently ran her hand through her son's hair.

"You know it." Zeke continued his examination and cleaned up where the hoof had sliced through Doug's skin. He was bleeding from the ear, but both his pupils were reactive. Zeke would try to control the swelling with IV medication. While he worked and talked to calm Doug, the cows were let out of the milkers, and the next portion of the herd was ushered in. Elaine's whistle and shouts as cows bunched together at one stall were background noise to his constant evaluation of his patient. At that point, all he could do was keep Doug comfortable. Once they got him into the ambulance, he'd start an IV. Although the dairy was clean, he and Doug were literally at the ass end of a cow. And the plop of a cow pie in the next milking station saturated the air with the flower fresh smell of cow shit.

It seemed like an eternity before the ambulance arrived, but when he checked his watch, it was the average response time.

"Hey, Zeke," one of the crew announced as they entered the barn, striding toward Zeke and Doug.

"Evan. Mark." He gave the ambulance crew a run down on injuries, and once they had Doug transferred to the gurney, he issued his orders. "I'll need an IV started, Ringers." Zeke also gave Evan the dosage of Toradol that he wanted to be administered. The non-narcotic pain reliever would help Doug reduce the swelling without conflicting with anything the attending surgeon would give him.

Dana came out of the barn as the team slid Doug into the ambulance. "I'll be heading to Rapid right behind you."

Zeke nodded. "We'll go in through emergency to get him admitted and up to the surgical floor, but you can just go up to surgery."

"Let me know what's happening when you can."

"You know I will. Can you have Elaine or Charlie bring my truck to Rapid?"

"Sure." Dana agreed and headed back into the barn. He buttoned up the door and waited until Evan and Mark had the bus turned around. Then he checked the IV and noticed the relaxation of Doug's features. The medication was helping. Zeke smiled down at Doug. "This will be something you laugh at in about six to eight weeks." When his jaw was no longer wired shut.

Doug lifted his eyes and gave Zeke a look that could wither cement.

Zeke chuckled, "Too soon?" Yup. That look would definitely nuke a sidewalk into dust.

FINISHING WITH HIS LAST PATIENT, Zeke ambled down to Jeremiah's office. It had been a hell of a week, starting with his Tuesday morning run to Rapid with Doug. The man was back home, and his jaw was banded shut. He went out and ensured everyone knew how to cut the bands if Doug got sick. Aspirating on one's own vomit wasn't a good way to die, and it could happen with a wired jaw.

It had been a steady stream of flu, colds, bronchitis, and minor aches and pains. Yesterday he broke away and headed out to the Marshall ranch. There was only one patient at the clinic, and they were there for PT, as Adam had mentioned. He ensured everyone at the ranch had access to his cell phone number and agreed to drive out on Monday, Wednesday, and Friday afternoons to see anyone who needed to be seen. The flu strain was a rabid bitch that year, taking people down right and left. Most folks tried to gut through the symptoms. When it got to be too much, Zeke took over and mandated rest and hydration, gave them over-the-counter meds for aches and pains, and watched over his people. Three patients had to go to Belle to be admitted. All were doing better, but damn, the season was just getting started. He thanked God he had a strong constitution and rarely fell ill.

He knocked on Jeremiah's door jamb as a courtesy. If he was doing his notes, Zeke didn't want to interrupt.

Jeremiah glanced up. "Hey. Done for the day?"

"Pretty much. I still have to dictate my notes. Did you get a chance to look at the job description?" They'd finished the paperwork, and Guardian had smoothed over any ruffled feathers in the state's bureaucratic machinery. They had the green light to put the job out for applications.

"I did, and I have some concerns. Where are you going to find someone with an insurance data-input background? You've eliminated everyone in at least a three-hundred-mile radius. I'd recommend taking that out."

Zeke dropped into one of the big comfy chairs in Jeremiah's office, not one of the hard bust-your-ass chairs in front of his desk. "Someone who needs a job has those qualifications."

Jeremiah chuckled. "You know, if I didn't know any better, I'd swear your degree was in social work."

"What can I say?" He shrugged.

"That you have a heart of gold, and you're probably one of the nicest people in the county." Jeremiah leaned back in his chair and plopped his cowboy boots onto the corner of his desk.

"I remember a time you couldn't stand the sight of me."

Jeremiah shook his head. "Not true. I just didn't like you very much. You had eyes for my woman."

Zeke snorted. "And she only had eyes for you. Lucky son of a bitch."

"Don't I know it? Who are you rescuing this time?"

"You know her." Zeke rolled his eyes, defending Stephanie before Jeremiah had a chance to say something about her. "She's a nice person."

"I'm sure she is, but who are we talking about?"

"Stephanie Howard." Zeke watched Jeremiah for any reaction.

His friend's brows drew together. "I thought she'd left. I haven't seen her in, hell, months." Jeremiah narrowed his eyes. "Why did you feel it necessary to tell me she's nice?"

"She's still here, needs a job, and has the experience."

Jeremiah cocked his head. "Are you avoiding my question or becoming selectively hard of hearing?"

"From what I've been told, she has a reputation around town." Zeke leaned forward and placed his elbows on his knees. "I don't want that to be an issue. She's had a rough go of it and needs a break." He wouldn't go into the details of what he'd overheard.

"As long as she's qualified, is a good receptionist, and can input all this admin shit into the system, let's hire her to take this crap off our laps."

Zeke smiled. "Listen to you. You don't have that many patients that aren't Guardians. You have no idea how much work this insurance and billing system is for me."

"I have my fair share, and don't whine, Zeke. It isn't very becoming." Jeremiah dodged the pen Zeke grabbed from the side table and chucked in his direction. Laughing, he picked up the pen and placed it on his desk. "Let's open the position announcement for one week and hire her to start on the first of February. Sound good?"

"No interview?" That was weird.

"It seems you've already done that, or you wouldn't have put the qualifier in the job description preventing anyone else from applying." Jeremiah's eyebrow lifted.

"Guess I have. Okay. I'll get it posted." Zeke could live with that. He stood and headed to his own office.

Jeremiah chuckled. "Should be interesting."

Zeke stopped and looked back at Jeremiah. "What?"

The man shook his head and waved Zeke off. "Nothing. Just talking to myself."

"You know, some people think that makes a person crazy."

Jeremiah laughed. "Not even close, my friend. Believe me. I know crazy."

7

Stephanie sat up, putting the book she'd been reading onto the small side table she'd found upstairs in the attic. The fireplace warmed the front room, and the old furnace took the chill off the rest of the house. The sound of a truck outside was curious. Declan didn't usually get many visitors. Unless one of his one-and-done girls had found her way back. Steph smiled despite herself. That wouldn't be funny, but Declan was courting disaster by bringing them to his home.

She moved to the window facing Declan's house and parted the curtains she'd salvaged from a trunk upstairs. Zeke got out of the truck and glanced from Declan's house to the old place. She blinked and dropped the curtains when he started her way.

Fear gripped her instantly. She reached for her hair, the curls were riotous, as usual, and she didn't have a lick of makeup on. "No. Stop it." She drew a deep breath. *You don't have to be perfect. You don't have to freak out.*

She jumped when he knocked, even though she was expecting it. Taking another deep breath, she walked to the door and opened it. "Hi?"

He smiled. "Not on crutches anymore?"

"Oh, no. I'm not. Did you come to get them?" She opened the door a bit wider.

"No, but if you aren't using them anymore, I'll take them back. May I come in for a minute?"

Stephanie gasped. "Of course, I'm sorry. Please, come in. Can I take your coat?" She opened the door wider, and he stepped in, dwarfing the small living room. She was reminded again of how big the doctor was. As he shrugged out of his down-filled jacket, her attention was caught by the size of his arms, which were as thick as her thighs. He'd make two of Presley. Her gaze traveled the length of his big body. He was magnificent ... Whoa, no. She wasn't going to go there. The last time she felt attracted to a man, she'd ended up in trouble. She took his coat and placed it on one of the wooden pegs mounted by the door. "Would you like some coffee or tea?"

"Thank you. Tea, whatever you have is fine."

"Please have a seat." She motioned to the small love seat and the recliner in the front room. He turned to take one, and she slipped into the old kitchen, pulling some Earl Grey out of the cupboard and fixing two mugs of tea. "Do you take cream or sugar?"

"Neither, thank you," his reply came from the front room.

She carried the mugs out and handed him his. "So, if you didn't come for the crutches, what did you come for?" She blinked, then shook her head. "That sounded rude, didn't it? I'm so sorry."

Zeke laughed, and the rumbling sound rolled around the small front room. "No, not at all. I came to talk to you about that position I mentioned when you were in the clinic the other night."

Stephanie sat down with her teacup. "I'm listening."

Zeke pulled the little tea tag up and down before he spoke. "I talked to Doctor Wheeler, and we wrote the position description so only someone with your background could qualify for the job. Basically, the job is yours if you want it. You can start on the first of February."

Stephanie closed her eyes and clasped her hands

together. "Thank you," she whispered the words. Her eyes flew open, and she immediately told him, "I promise I'll be much more put together than this." She waved at the jeans and sweater she was wearing. The sweater was one of hers from high school that was boxed up and stashed upstairs. The new jeans Declan had purchased for her in Belle.

"Actually, what you're wearing is perfect. Jeans are the standard around here. Anything fancier, and we might make the patients feel uncomfortable."

"Oh. Okay." She had a box full of old sweaters. She'd be okay until she had a couple of paychecks under her belt and could buy some more clothes. "I appreciate the opportunity."

"You might regret it when you get a load of the system and the amount of work you'll be doing. You didn't ask about the pay."

She let a nervous smile flash across her face. "I don't care. Anything I can get at this point is wonderful." Zeke shrugged and told her the amount she'd be getting per hour. Her mouth dropped, "You're joking."

"Not in the slightest. We've run that practice by ourselves for years. You'll have a lot of work to do. I need my digital filing system cleaned up. Plus, we both have records that need to be staged after you ensure they've all been scanned in and sent to the state. Then there's the state's administrative paperwork. Part of my pay comes from the state, and they're ridiculous with the amount of paperwork they require. I don't know how many times they've tracked me down to hound me for my quarterly reports or made me redo a document because I didn't tick a box. Believe me, you'll earn every penny of the money."

"I can't wait to start." Stephanie let the wonderful feeling of happiness inside her rise to the surface and smiled.

"You'll have to sign a nondisclosure statement. You can't say anything about the patients or what goes on at the clinic. That letter is in the package."

"Of course. I would never discuss anyone else's business. I hate gossip," she spat the last words out. She glanced at him. "Sorry."

"Don't be. We're in the same boat on that point. I brought out the employment packet. If you could fill in the information, I'll get it started as soon as we close out the application period." He reached in his coat and pulled out an envelope. Instead of handing it to her, he placed it on the coffee table. "My cell phone number is in there, too. Everyone in the county has it. Call me if you have any questions."

She'd moved to pick up the envelope but stopped. "I don't have a cell phone. I can buy one if I need one." Presley had taken her phone from her, and she hadn't wasted any money buying a new one.

"No need. It isn't a requirement for the job." Zeke took a sip of his coffee. "Earl Grey."

Stephanie flashed a smile at him. "You like tea?"

"My mom is a self-proclaimed tea snob. Although she now drinks it iced since she moved to Florida, so she's really not that much of a snob."

Stephanie laughed. "Not many men I know enjoy tea." None that she knew, actually.

Zeke shrugged. "I'm an enigma." He took another sip. "I'll go and let you take a look at the papers. Have Declan bring them in, and I'll pick them up from the Bit and Spur."

She shook her head. "Stay and enjoy your tea. And you don't need to come out to fetch the papers. I can bring them into town."

Zeke leaned back in his chair. "I thought you'd left town. I hadn't seen you around for months."

"I've been staying here, keeping to myself. The town of Hollister and I have history."

"Anything I should know about for work? I don't want to pry, but ..."

"No. Nothing that would prohibit me from working. Just a lot of drama that never should have happened." She didn't want to get any further into what happened and prayed he'd leave it at that.

He nodded. "All right, then, I look forward to working with you, Stephanie. Thank you for the tea." He stood and headed to the door.

"Zeke?"

He turned at the door with his coat in his hand and looked at her questioningly. "Thank you. I won't let you down."

Zeke smiled and slid into his jacket. He grabbed the crutches propped by the door and lifted them before saying, "I don't think that's in your nature." He opened the door and walked out before she could process his words.

She stood and walked to the door, pulling the curtains back. *I have a job.* She closed her eyes and dropped her forehead onto the cold glass window. Maybe things were finally looking up.

STEPHANIE LAID the last sweater she'd washed on a kitchen chair in front of the fireplace to dry. She'd been so excited about Zeke's visit that she'd tackled several more boxes from the upstairs storage area that had her name on them. She'd found some usable clothes, her cheerleading uniform, and several pictures from her old bedroom, including one with her and Andrew. She'd left that upstairs. A picture of her mom and dad sat on the mantle, along with a picture of her and Declan.

She sat down with a fresh cup of tea and read over the application she'd filled out, ensuring she'd completed each section, when she heard another vehicle pull up outside. Glancing at the clock, a tendril of unease raced along her spine. It was dark, Declan was at the bar, and no one should be there.

There was a moment of silence before she heard the sound of a vehicle door shutting. Steph made her way to the window. She pulled the curtain back with shaking hands and flipped on the porch light. What in the world?

She opened the door. "Gen? Are you looking for … Declan?" She had no idea why Andrew's fiancée would be there. She was grasping for any reason and came up blank.

"No, actually, I came to see you." Gen smiled as she mounted the steps. "May I come in?"

"Oh, sorry, sure. Come in." Steph stood back. "Sorry about this, I'm drying sweaters, and they've taken over the entire room. We could talk in the kitchen?"

"That's fine. I love your hair that way." Gen stepped into the house.

"It looks like Shirley Temple got caught in a windstorm." Stephanie laughed. "At least that's what my mom used to say. Let me take your coat."

"I like the curls. Seriously." Gen followed her into the kitchen after Steph hung her coat on the same peg Zeke's coat had occupied earlier.

"Would you like some tea?" Steph stopped. "Can I ask why you're here? I mean, I haven't done or said anything to anyone. If someone said otherwise ..." She rubbed her forehead with her fingers. "I can't do that again. There were so many things they said about me that weren't true."

Gen's face went blank. "Oh, God. No, that has nothing to do with why I'm here. I was visiting with Declan because I wanted to use the Bit and Spur to host a reception for the town after Andrew and I get married. He suggested that I talk to you because I wanted decorations. We'll do the food at the diner, but I really want the Spur to look awesome, you know, fairy lights and—"

"White satin from the center of the ceiling draping out to the corners covering the beams," Stephanie interjected. She caught herself and back peddled. "Oh, sorry."

"No, don't be! That's exactly what I want. Tables with skirts and maybe the wall with the dart boards covered with the same white satin."

"What about a head table where the band plays on the stage?"

"Yes, that's a brilliant idea. I have a budget of fifteen hundred dollars for decorations and such. Is it possible to transform the Spur into a reception hall with that much money?"

"Wow. With that kind of money, you can do a lot. When are you planning the reception?"

"The last Sunday of the month. Declan said we could decorate all day and have the event at night. He isn't open on Monday. Drew and I are getting married in Denver. My folks, his father, and a few others will be there. We'll do all the hoity-toity things there, wedding pictures and such, but we both want to celebrate with our friends in town. I know there isn't much time to pull it together, but I've been so busy with the venue and issues in Denver that I let the reception bubble on the back burner. Can you help me? Please?"

Steph's thoughts about transforming the Spur screamed to a halt. "Wait, me?"

"Yes. Would you please be in charge of decorating for the reception? Everyone in town is invited, and I'd love for them to see there's no animosity between the three of us." Gen reached out her hand. "Ciera is doing all the food. Declan will run the bar, but I need someone to ensure everything else is done."

"Ah, sure, I can do it, but are you sure you want me to take care of everything? You don't really know me."

"No, but Drew does. He knows both of you were in the same position, and the rumors that were floating couldn't be true. You're not that kind of person."

Steph wrapped her arms around herself. She wasn't, but that didn't mean people would believe it after all that time. "And you believe him?"

Gen smiled and said softly, "I trust Drew with my life, and we both know what desperation can make a person do." Gen stared at her. "Please, will you help us? Me?"

Steph drew a deep breath and nodded. "I sealed my fate by allowing those rumors to persist without defending myself. I can handle the town thinking what they will about me, but I'm so glad you and Andrew believe differently. Would you like that cup of tea now?"

"I'd love one." Gen sat at the kitchen table on one of the two chairs that weren't used as a clothesline to dry her sweaters.

Stephanie put the kettle on the old range and cranked on the burner.

"Oh, what about a cake?" Steph grabbed a small pad of paper and headed to the drawer with her pencils and pens.

"Allison's mom is making it. Two sheet pans and a small one, Drew and I can cut. I'm told smashing cake in each other's faces is a great way to start the dessert course."

Stephanie rolled her eyes. "I never got that. You've invested thousands in your gown, spent all day on makeup and hair, and then you get a buttercream facial from the one who's supposed to love, honor, cherish, and protect you. It had to be a man who came up with the idea."

Gen laughed. "I'd bet on that, too. Ciera is doing heavy appetizers. She'll need a twelve-foot table and will bring the food before the event. She and Corrie will keep the trays stocked during the night. Declan said he'd clear the beer coolers, so we can use them for food."

"Yeah, he has coolers downstairs he can transfer the beer into. What about chafing dishes?"

"No. Nothing with an open flame. Declan said that was a big no-no."

Steph nodded. "I can see that. Okay, so I'll go down to Rapid this weekend, get everything, and work on cutting the fabric to length. Oh, what are your colors?"

"White and red. Poinsettias and roses."

"Perfect. I can get some silk or paper flowers to intersperse along the white and pin the material around the tables to form skirts."

"Fantastic idea. Thank you so much for doing this." Gen reached into her back pocket and pulled out an envelope. "There's the money."

"I'll give you an itemized list of expenditures and the receipts."

"I don't need that." Gen shook her head.

"I do." Steph shrugged. "I want to ensure I earn your trust, not just because of what Andrew thinks of me, but of how I act. Does that make sense?" She had a lot of mileage to cover to redeem herself in the community.

"Yes. I get it. I opened my diner and set out to prove my mother wrong. I showed her I could succeed and didn't need to use any connections to do it. She's my greatest critic."

"Oh, that sounds like a story." Stephanie got two mugs down because the cup she'd used earlier was in the living room. She didn't want to navigate her impromptu clotheslines only to move right back out. She made the tea and handed it to Gen. "Milk or sugar?"

"Neither, thanks. This is perfect." Gen took the mug.

"Can you think of anything else we need to do to the place?"

Imagining the bar in her mind, Stephanie walked through it and nodded. "The dance floor. Do you want tables, or do you want it clear for dancing?"

"Clear. I want everyone to mingle, not sit down and grow roots. It'll encourage people to come and go that way, too." She took a sip of her tea and groaned. "Do you know how long it's been since I've sat down and visited with someone? I'm not abused in any conceivable fashion. I had no idea there were five million things to do for a wedding. Well, make that ten million because I have to keep undoing what my mother tries to do. I swear, I had to tell the wedding planner if she changed one more thing based on anything my mother asks for, I'd fire her."

Stephanie blinked and snapped her mouth shut. "Your mom was changing what you've done?"

Gen swung her eyes up from the tea mug. "You haven't heard about my mother?"

Stephanie shook her head. "After being the topic of gossip, I avoid it at all costs. The last time I was in your diner with Allison and Kathy for lunch, Ciera dropped a couple of the guy's lunch orders on the floor. That started Allison and Kathy talking about her. I made up an excuse and left. I haven't been back to town since."

"What?"

Stephanie shook her head. "See, what they said wasn't bad, just that they thought she had it tough, you know? But it just struck me to the core because I've been the one destroyed during casual conversation. And if I'm being honest, I can't do that anymore. So I came out here and have only left once with Declan, and we went to Belle."

Gen reached across the table. "I am so sorry. I've

been lost in my own world. I didn't notice you'd stopped coming to town."

Steph cocked her head. "Why should you have noticed?"

"Because that's what people in Hollister do. They watch out for other people." Gen smiled. "You're part of the town. The past is long over. Don't hide here. People in Hollister are decent if you give them a chance, and I've learned they judge a person by what they do *now*. The past is a slippery slope for a hell of a lot of people."

"Do you really think so?" Stephanie lifted an eyebrow.

"That's what I've seen. Maybe the toxicity has lessened since you've been gone. It has been a while."

She wasn't so sure. Steph stared down at the pencil in her hand. "Is it okay if I talk to Ciera and have her come show me where the table would be best for her?"

"Absolutely. And if you want to ride down to Rapid with her and Scott, they're going on Wednesday. Corrie will cover Ciera's shift, and I'll take Corrie's. Ciera is still working mornings to early afternoon."

Stephanie blinked. "Why wouldn't she be? Did you change the hours to the diner?"

"Oh, no. Ciera and Scott got married. They popped over to the justice of the peace. Which, if I could do all this over, I would do in a heartbeat." Gen rolled her eyes.

"No, you wouldn't. Admit it. All the fancy dresses and flowers make you happy." Stephanie could see the sparkle in Gen's eyes. The woman was glowing with happiness.

Gen smiled wide. "I never thought I'd be that girly girl, you know? But I tried on at least thirty wedding dresses." She laughed and shook her head. "There's so much to do."

Stephanie joined in her laughter. "Well, the decorations and set up for the reception is one less thing you need to worry about. I wanted something to keep me occupied. Looks like I got it."

"What's that old saying, don't ask for more than you can handle?"

Stephanie nodded. "I can handle it, though. I promise. Thank you for trusting me." She'd said those words twice today, and that really felt good. Soul deep good.

After Gen left about a half hour later, Stephanie added a couple of logs to the fire and wound her way through her drying sweaters. She sunk into the warm brown leather of the oversized recliner her father had loved and sighed, closing her eyes. *You're going to be okay.* For the first time in a long time, she actually believed that statement could be true.

8

Zeke finished his coffee. "Where's Ciera today?" he asked Corrie as she dropped a splash of coffee into his cup.

"She and Scott are going to Rapid to get things for the reception."

Zeke cocked his head. "What reception?"

"Doc, where have you been? Gen and Andrew are throwing a reception at the Spur this weekend or Monday, depending on the weather. Ciera and I are cooking the food, and Stephanie Howard is doing the decorations."

"Decorations? What like crepe paper streamers?" Carson Schmidt chuckled.

Edna snorted from her booth. "Not likely. I heard from Gen that Stephanie has some fantastic ideas. I can't wait to see it. Steph's a good kid." Edna waved her cup at Corrie. "Can I get a refill?"

"Coming right up." Corrie hustled over her way.

"I thought she'd left," Carson mused. "She's one hell of a looker." His tone grated on Zeke's nerves.

"She's a nice person." His tone cautioned Carson.

The man did a double take. "Didn't say she wasn't. Said she was a looker." Carson narrowed his eyes. "You okay?"

"I'm fine." Zeke nodded.

The bell rang, and a blast of cold air filled the café. "Hi, Corrie." Stephanie stood at the door, bundled up.

"Come in and warm up. I'll bring you a cup of coffee and let Ciera and Scott know you're here."

"Tea," Zeke said, and Stephanie's head snapped in his direction.

A radiant smile spread across her face as she greeted him. "Hi."

"Tea it is," Corrie said as she entered the kitchen. Stephanie took off her knit hat, and her hair fell in a riot of curls. Zeke motioned to the bar stool next to him, and Steph made her way over. "Hey, Miss Edna." Steph waved as she sat down.

"Stephanie. Heard you have a decorating job. You call me if you need help."

Zeke kept his eyes down and forced himself not to smile. He wasn't sure how much actual help Edna would be.

"Thank you, that's sweet. I will definitely shout if I need help." She turned as Corrie put the tea down in front of her. "Thank you."

"No problem. Let me go tell Ciera you're here."

"I'm early. I was excited. Tell her absolutely no rush." Stephanie unwrapped the tea bag and poured steaming hot water over it.

"Will do, honey." Corrie floated back into the kitchen.

"I heard you had some nice plans to decorate the Spur." Zeke took a drink of his coffee.

"I do have plans, but I'm going to alter them to match whatever supplies I can find in Rapid."

"You do your hair differently?" Carson leaned forward so he could see past Zeke.

"Hi, Carson. I left it curly."

"I like it, but straight was good, too." Carson gave her a smile that Zeke wanted to slap off his face.

"Good to know she meets with your approval, Carson," Zeke said dryly.

"What? Hey, no, I didn't mean it that way. I was just saying she looks good."

Stephanie gave him a quick smile but didn't say anything.

"Man, I'm going back to the store before I step in it harder." Carson got up and dropped the money for his breakfast. "Stephanie, it was good to see you again. Edna, keep it cool."

"In this weather, how in the world would I keep it any other way?" Edna guffawed as Carson left.

"Sorry for my friend. I think I'll have to re-educate him on how to flirt." Zeke chuckled.

"Was that what he was trying to do? Flirt?" Stephanie's eyes grew large. "Classes are needed."

Zeke reminded himself to thank Carson for taking himself out of the competition. The woman next to him might not know it, but he was going to take her out on a date.

"What do you think will be the hardest things to find?" Zeke drove the conversation toward her day.

"Ah, probably silk and paper flowers. Hopefully, the poinsettias will be on discount since it's after Christmas. Roses are always in demand, so I might buy paper and make them myself. Not a great option, but doable."

"I'm sure whatever you do will be fine."

Stephanie shook her head. "I want it to be perfect for Gen and Andrew."

"That's why everything will be fine." Zeke leaned over and bumped her shoulder lightly.

Stephanie froze for a moment before smiling. That time, the smile went to her eyes and made them sparkle, unlike the smile she'd given Carson. He patted himself on the back. "Thank you."

Ciera bounced through the kitchen. "Are you ready, Stephanie? Scott is warming up the truck. We can go through the kitchen."

"Be right there." Stephanie took a final sip of her tea before reaching into her purse. "It was nice talking with you."

"I've got it." Zeke motioned to the tea.

"Are you sure?"

"Absolutely. Have fun in Rapid."

"Thank you. I think I will." She beamed a smile at him and darted after Ciera.

CIERA AND SCOTT waved as the truck and trailer pulled away from the Bit and Spur, and Declan grunted as he picked up the last box of decorations. "Did you buy out the party store?"

Stephanie tossed her curls over her shoulder and bent down to grab two bags perched on a snow drift.

"I didn't go to a party store." She'd gone to a fabric store, a big box store, a hobby store, and a lighting store, but not a party store. "You're supplying the party juice, remember?"

"Hey, when someone wants an open bar, who am I to complain?" Declan put the box behind the bar with the rest of her purchases. "Have you talked to Gen lately? That blizzard is supposed to hit on Monday. Not sure if they're going to risk having a get-together."

"I talked to her this morning. They're watching the weather, and all the out-of-town guests are leaving from Denver, not making the trip back here, so it'll just be the locals coming to the reception." Steph followed Declan to the stairs and waited for him to turn the corner before she carried the bags in her hands down into the basement.

"Stay here. I'll get the rest of it. You can organize it how you want it." Declan made fast work of climbing the stairs two at a time. She was digging through the many strings of fairy lights she'd purchased when she heard Declan descending the stairs again. "Can I use your staple gun? I forgot to buy one."

"Of course." The deep baritone didn't belong to her brother, and it startled her. She twisted violently and lost her balance, ass-planting on the cement floor. "Hey, are you all right?" Zeke sat the boxes he was carrying down and made his way over to her.

She groaned and looked up at the handsome doctor who'd made her morning. Few people had faith in her, and his kind words that morning warmed her throughout the day.

"Ah ... No. My pride is bruised." She accepted a hand and rubbed her backside when she had her feet under her.

"I don't have a medical remedy for that." Zeke smiled at her. "I'm sorry. I didn't mean to startle you. Declan is upstairs. Phil is here for his nightly beer."

"Is it five already?" Stephanie blinked up at him.

"It is. I'll go grab the rest of the boxes."

"I can do that," she offered to his retreating back.

"Nope, I got it. You go back to bruising your pride. Doctor's orders."

She rolled her eyes. Seemed like she never was on the right foot around Zeke. The butterflies in her stomach made an appearance again. They seemed to flit about whenever Zeke was nearby. She felt her face warm. Maybe she was reading into constantly bumping into the doctor. It was a small town, after all. Still, he was there. Stephanie smiled and allowed herself the hope that it wasn't random. She pushed the boxes Zeke had put down over to the corner with the rest of her decorations.

A few minutes later, she heard him talking as he walked down the stairs. "Just wanted you to know that the state has officially hired you. Congratulations and commiserations. I'm happy you're coming to work with us and thrilled that I don't have to do any more billing paperwork."

"What are the commiserations for?" She accepted a small box from him and peeked inside before moving it to the other boxes' far side.

"For having to clean up years of files, paperwork, and administrative bunk that neither Jeremiah nor I wanted to do."

Stephanie laughed. "I'll be fine. That's called job security. Always something to do. Could you put that one down over there?" She pointed to the box in his grasp.

"You went all out on decorations, didn't you?" Zeke stacked the box where she asked him to put it.

"Yes and no. I found all the bargains I could. Gen wants it beautiful, and I'm going to try my best to give it to her." She put her hands on her hips and nodded as she surveyed her purchases.

"When are you going to put them up? Isn't

Declan open on Saturday night?" Zeke leaned against the cement block wall.

"After he closes. He's closing at ten as a favor to me. I'll be here all night, but it'll be worth it. That way, it'll be ready on Sunday if they need to move the reception up because of the storm." Stephanie smiled at him. "Can I buy you a drink? I'm done for the day."

Zeke cocked his head at her. "It just so happens I'm done, too. I'll take you up on that, but I'm buying."

She laughed. "Zeke, remember my brother owns this place. I'm not actually buying, but you would be."

"Oh, in that case, buy us a drink, by all means." Zeke followed her up the stairs, and as she turned to grab the string that switched off the light, she caught him staring at her backside. His eyes flashed up to hers, and his eyebrows lifted before he smiled and winked. The heat from the blood rushing to her cheeks was instantaneous. She clicked off the light and turned away a split second before letting a smile slip across her lips. The momentary joy of the casual flirtation faltered as Presley pushed his way back into her thoughts. No. She was done with him, and damn him, she wouldn't let him take the happiness of casual flirtation away from her.

"Declan, your sister is buying me a drink." Zeke walked out from behind the bar and sat down on a stool across from where Stephanie went to pull the beers.

Declan looked at his sister. "What did I tell you about feeding strays? If you give him that, this guy will keep coming around." Declan lifted his chin at Zeke while he washed out a beer glass.

"That's a promise." Zeke smiled at her, and she felt her cheeks flame again. She sat the beer down in front of Zeke and poured one for herself.

"Declan, I got the job." Stephanie walked around the end of the bar and hopped up onto the high barstool next to Zeke.

"He's going to be your boss, then?" Declan chuckled. "Good luck."

"Actually, no. Her boss is a woman in the billing department down in Belle Fourche. We're coworkers." Zeke took a drink of his beer.

"What?" Stephanie sat her beer down. "Isn't that strange?"

"It's perfect as far as I'm concerned." Zeke shrugged. "She'll come up once a quarter, but other than that, we're doing our own thing up here."

Declan moved down the bar as two more men came in, and Zeke glanced at her. "I like your hair that way, and I like it when you don't wear makeup."

Stephanie took a drink of her beer. "I'm not sure if that was a compliment or not."

Zeke's eyes widened. "It was meant as a compliment. You don't need makeup. You're beautiful without it."

Stephanie didn't quite know how to take that. A compliment, yes, but ... What was happening? She left the compliment alone but told him the truth, "I've decided it was time to be myself. I can't live up to other people's expectations."

"You shouldn't have to." Zeke nudged her with his elbow. "Anyone who wants to change who you are isn't someone you should be with."

Turning on her stool, Steph looked at him and took a deep breath, forcing herself to admit, "I agree. I was with a man who abused me. I was afraid to leave him, and it reached a point where I couldn't leave. Eventually, it got so bad that I ran away when I got the chance. That's why I came home." She watched his face for any reaction.

Zeke turned toward her, their knees touched, but he didn't shift to remove the contact. "Abusive relationships are a nightmare. I'm glad you were able to leave. I'm glad you're home." He held her gaze, and she stopped breathing for a moment. His eyes were so intensely blue. He was gorgeous and kind. *Presley was kind at first.* She drew back and averted her gaze.

"What happened just now?" Zeke's eyes narrowed. "What crossed your mind to make you afraid?"

Stephanie dropped her eyes and slowly spun her beer around on its coaster. "He messed me up. I have some lingering problems, but I'm working through them."

Zeke finished his beer and stood up in the small space between the barstools, towering over her. She stopped herself from shrinking back as he leaned down and whispered in her ear. "I'll wait for you."

She blinked and tried to say something, but he was gone, waving to Declan and walking out the door.

"What was that all about?" Declan made his way down the bar and retrieved the empty glass and coaster.

"What was what about?" She took a drink of her beer and leveled a gaze at her brother. She didn't ask about his bar bunnies, did she? Not that Zeke was a one-night stand type of guy. Or at least he didn't strike her as that type of guy. But did she know what type of man he was? She knew he'd been in town for years. Her brother liked him, and so did everyone else. The few times she'd been in town, no one had a bad word to say about him.

"All right, don't tell me." Declan rolled his eyes and headed to the sink. Stephanie spun her glass again. Maybe she would tell Declan. Someday, when she figured out exactly what was going on. Her eyes locked on the door. Zeke. *Don't get your hopes up*. She sighed and nodded her head. The doctor was flirting. It was nothing more than that.

9

Zeke pulled into the front of Gen's diner and parked his truck. The snow was deep and getting deeper, although the bulk of the weather was coming next week, according to the weather reports. He made his way into the diner and pulled his coat off, hanging it on the rack where several other customers' bulky winter jackets resided.

"Zeke, how goes it?" Deputy Ken Zorn said from his usual spot at the diner's counter.

Zeke sat down and glanced around at the few people in the diner. He nodded to those who smiled at him, then answered Ken, "It goes. Rather sparse in here today."

Ken nodded. "Good day to stay hunkered down

by the fire. Some of us can't do that, though."

"I put my chains on the truck yesterday. Figured why wait." If he had to go out on a house call, he didn't want to end up stranded in a drift or ditch. Besides, he was anticipating returning to Stephanie's house to pick up the employment forms in the next day or two. It was an excuse to see her. He'd lost sleep thinking about that woman. You'd think he'd learn, but something about her drew him like a bee to a honeycomb, especially since seeing her without makeup and wearing jeans and a tight sweater. The physical, coupled with the soft personality and warm heart, was an instant twenty out of ten for him. He hadn't felt that way about a woman since Eden, which was over before it began, thanks to Jeremiah's arrival in Hollister. That was a massive bruise to his ego.

"The storm is going to be a big one," Ken said, startling him from his musings.

He blinked back into the conversation. "Next week, right?" Zeke hadn't watched the news in a while, and radio reception was squat that morning, so he turned it off.

Ken shrugged. "Monday-ish. You know how these things go."

"Indeed, I do." He'd lived through enough South

Dakota winters to be prepared for the worst and always be prepared for the storms to come sooner or last longer than the meteorologists said they would.

Zeke smiled at Ciera, who appeared out of the kitchen and poured him a cup of coffee. "Lunch special is paella. No seafood, just chicken and sausage, but it's good and will warm you all the way through. It's just me today. It was so slow I told Corrie to go home. I have appetizers to make for the reception this afternoon. No sense both of us being here."

"I'll take a healthy serving of paella." Zeke could use a good meal. Mary Beth Thompson had a bad case of the flu and was running a fever, so her parents were taking her down to Belle. An ambulance wasn't needed, but the two-year-old was dehydrated, and he didn't have any pediatric IV equipment, which he'd have to rectify. He gave her some anti-nausea meds and told her mom to keep giving her sips of Pedialyte on the way to the hospital.

"Got it. Yours will be right out, too, Ken."

The deputy waved her off. "Bring mine out when you bring his." He dipped his head in Zeke's direction. "Need to talk to him, anyway."

"You got it." Ciera smiled and headed over to

refill the other diner's coffee cups.

Zeke turned his head toward Ken. "What are we talking about?"

"Three men camping on Hollister's land." Ken took a sip of his coffee.

"Ah, the Thompsons. Problems?"

"Nope. It would have been good to know they were there, though." Ken gave him a sideways look.

"Ah, well. At least Mitch got the truck fixed. They're looking for work." Zeke had paid the repair bill. Phil Granger had done the best he could with the truck, and it would run well for the foreseeable future.

"He found work. Mitch is starting at the processing plant on Monday. Hollisters had just hired someone on the recommendation of Frank Marshall to fill the vacant position they had at the ranch. Kerry said he'd have Mitch doing janitorial and handyman stuff until they get busy in the spring, but it's honest work."

"Good of them to find him a spot. They've been on hard times." He wasn't going to ask anything further, especially when Ken mentioned Frank Marshall. If there were a Guardian issue he needed to worry about, Adam Cassidy would have given him the information. His new friend and his wife had extended the stay with her sister. Adam had called to make sure Zeke could handle both the ranch and the locals until the storm passed, and Zeke had no problem driving out to the ranch three times a week. Not that there was much to do. A rope burn, twisted ankle, and, of course, colds and the flu were everywhere. He also completed a nervous dad check on a perfectly healthy little girl. Zeke chuckled. Dixon Marshall loved that baby girl something fierce. She'd never be allowed to date. Poor thing.

Ciera put two massive bowls filled with rice, meat, and veggies in front of them. He took a bite and rolled his eyes to the heavens. The saffron didn't overpower the dish, and the spices sang on his tongue. "So good."

Ken nodded and shoveled another bite into his mouth. When he finished chewing, Ken cleared his throat. "The Thompsons need better shelter than that fifth wheel for this storm." Ken rolled his shoulders.

"I figured. Planned on looking into that this afternoon."

"Good call." Ken broke off a piece of sourdough bread and slathered it in butter.

Zeke followed suit but limited his butter to a smear. "I'll drive out today and tell them to bring the

RV into town. They can park in the back lot of the clinic. The lot is level. I'm not sure if there are any empty places around town." He'd pay rent for the first month for the men if they could find something. If not, he could take them in. It wouldn't be the first time he'd helped people out. They ate in silence for a moment.

Ken jabbed the air with his thumb toward the far side of town. "One of the Marshall cabins over yonder is always dark. Someone moved into the other."

Zeke nodded and took another bite of his lunch. He could take a run out to the Marshalls and ask Mr. Marshall if he could rent the cabin until it was needed. If he got the go-ahead, he'd swing by the Thompsons' and help them move the RV and settle in.

The bell on the door jingled again, and Zeke glanced toward it. He smiled at the riot of blonde curls that emerged from the hood of the oversized jacket. Ken glanced at him and did a double take before he shook his head. "She's trouble," he murmured.

Zeke snapped his attention to his friend. "Based on what? Rumors? I think you should mind your own business. You don't know what happened."

"And you do?"

Zeke glanced at Stephanie as she shrugged off her coat. "I most certainly do." Catching Stephanie's attention, he motioned her to the stool next to him. "Stephanie, have a seat. Hot tea?"

The smile across her face faltered when she glanced at Ken Zorn. "Are you sure?"

Zeke smiled. "Positive. Ciera, would you get Stephanie some hot tea?"

"On it. Herbal or caffeinated, Steph?"

"Caffeine, *please*. Hey, Ken."

"Steph." Ken nodded and resumed eating. Zeke would have liked to slap the back of Ken's head for his behavior, but he ignored the man and hoped Stephanie would, too. She dropped into the seat beside Zeke.

"Ready to start work?" Zeke saw Ken pause with his fork halfway to his mouth.

"I am, but first, I need to get through Gen and Andrew's reception. Honestly, I don't know what I was thinking."

Ken snorted. "That bothers you, does it?"

Stephanie leaned forward. "No, Ken, it doesn't. Your aunt lied about me a long time ago, and I didn't say a word, but damn it, I didn't cheat on Andrew, and you can go screw yourself if you think I did.

Your Aunt Donna hated me, and you know it. She spread those rumors, and if you look at things honestly, you'd see it. Gen asked *me* to decorate the Bit and Spur for *their* reception, which I agreed to do because I like her. Andrew and I have no problems. It is a lot of work, and *that* was what I meant by I didn't know what I was thinking. Now, would you please take your unjustified judgment and shove it where the sun doesn't shine?"

She sat back and pulled her hands down to her lap. Zeke noticed how bad they shook as she clenched them together and smiled before tossing Ken's words back at him. "That bothers you, does it?"

Ken snorted dismissively and continued to eat. Obviously not changing his mind about Stephanie. Well, that was something Ken would have to get over, or not, depending on how deep the deputy's emotions ran. If things went the way Zeke was hoping, he and Ken would have a heart-to-heart in the not-too-distant future. But he was taking his time. Stephanie was as skittish as a cat in a room full of rocking chairs. He wouldn't be one to snip her tail, and he'd make sure no one else did either. When he had the right. Which he hoped would be sooner rather than later.

Ciera came out with a little pot of hot water and

a fancy teacup. “Here you go, Steph. I have three trays of chocolate trifles finished and frozen. They thaw perfectly in a refrigerator and will be ready for the reception. Can I take them over to the Spur? Cody and Scott will get into them if I keep them here.” The woman laughed and shook her head. “They both have a sweet tooth.”

Stephanie looked grateful for the interruption. “I can take the trays over when I’m finished here.”

“Are you sure?” Ciera asked. “I can do it.”

“No need. I’m going over to finish cutting the last of the fabric to length. I’ve made the flower arrangements; I know where the fairy lights go, and I’ve organized the table placements. I did a running seam on the skirts and pulled and tacked it, so the pleats would stay. I’ll attach them to the tablecloths; boom, everything comes together. All I have to do is put everything in place.”

“I can help.” Ciera offered as she grabbed the coffee pot from the station behind the bar.

“Honestly, I have it all planned out, and I’ll be fine. It won’t take but an hour or so to get everything set up but thank you for the offer.” Steph smiled and took a sip of her tea. “What smells so wonderful?”

“Paella.” Zeke and Ciera said at the same time.

“Want some?” Ciera pointed to the kitchen.

"Yes, please, but not that much. Maybe a quarter that size?" Stephanie pointed to Zeke's nearly empty plate.

"You got it. I'll be right back." She headed to the two occupied tables and refreshed the other patrons' coffee cups before stepping back into the kitchen.

Ken Zorn wiped his mouth and removed money from his wallet before he stood up. "Zeke, you'll take care of the Thompsons?"

"I've got it. I'll call if there are any issues you need to be aware of."

"All right. Steph." Ken dipped his head and headed to the coat rack to retrieve his winter coat.

"He hates me," Steph whispered as she brought her tea to her lips. "He's branded me with a scarlet letter."

"His loss," Zeke said. "Do you need help with decorations?"

"No, I'm fine, really. I have Declan's staple gun and a sturdy ladder. It's just a matter of putting things in place." She chuckled. "I even drew a diagram of where each piece goes and numbered them. Declan thinks I'm insane, but I like things to flow logically."

"That bodes well for our practices." Zeke nodded in the direction of the clinic. "I've scanned in all your documents and forwarded them to HR. We're ready for you to start on the first."

"I look forward to it. I didn't realize how much I missed being busy." Steph smiled and thanked Ciera when she delivered a smaller portion of paella and collected Ken's money and dirty dishes.

Steph glanced over at him after Ciera left. "Who are the Thompsons?"

"A family that needs some help." Zeke wouldn't go further into it.

"Anything I can do?" Stephanie glanced up at him. Her expression was sincere and open.

"Not right now, but if there is, I'll let you know."

"Please do. I can help clean, babysit, or maybe bring them some food. I don't have much, but if they need anything, I'll give what I can." Zeke watched her take a bite of the paella and absorbed the moment. He noted her obvious concern without prying for details he didn't want to divulge. The woman had next to nothing, was coming out of a horrid relationship, yet wanted to help people she didn't know. *That* told him more about her character than any gossip would ever reveal. Yes, she was everything he'd hoped she was. Attractive? God, yes. But her beauty radiated from the inside, and without the make-up and fancy clothes, it beamed brightly.

Zeke lowered his voice and asked, "Has anyone ever told you how special you are?"

She froze. Her eyes slid to him as if to check if he was being sarcastic. She shook her head. "I'm not."

He picked up his cup and smiled at her. "That's where you're wrong, Stephanie Howard."

She shook her head and took a bite of her lunch. When she finished, she replied. "Is it bad that I don't want to be special?"

"What is it you want to be?" He leaned in, and their elbows touched as they talked.

She didn't say anything for a long minute. Finally, she met his gaze. "I want to be free. Free of the past. Free to be me, to live life unafraid." She shrugged and looked at him. "What do you want?"

He sat his coffee cup down on the counter. He thought about that for a moment, giving the question the consideration it deserved. "Pie in the sky want?"

She nodded at him. "Aim for the heavens."

"I want a loving, committed relationship with someone I know is special. Someone like you."

Her mouth dropped open, and he smiled, chucking her on the chin. She snapped her jaw shut and stuttered, "Y-You don't know me."

"Not yet, but we'll get there." Zeke stood up and

dropped a twenty. Ciera passed by, and Zeke motioned to the money. "That's for Stephanie's lunch and mine."

"You got it. Bye, Doc."

"See you." He waved at the remaining diners and headed back to his truck. He needed to go out to the Marshall ranch. He didn't try to hide the smile that spread across his face. He'd become enamored with that woman. A cynical voice from somewhere inside his mind chimed in. *You're setting yourself up for another disaster.* God, he hoped not.

STEPHANIE BLINKED AT THE COUNTER. How did Zeke do that? Leave her breathless and confused and more than just a little curious.

"He's a good man, Steph." Ciera said as she picked up his dishes.

Stephanie jerked as if she'd been hit. "What?"

Ciera frowned and stopped in front of her. "He's a good man. You should get to know him. I really like the thought of him and you together."

Steph blinked. "I thought you were warning me to stay away."

Ciera put down the dishes in her hands and

came around the counter, sitting where Zeke had been moments before. "Why would I do that?"

"People around here think I'm a blight on polite society."

Ciera snorted. "No, they don't. The only thing I've ever heard about you is that your fancy clothes didn't make sense in Hollister. Edna said that, but no one has ever said anything bad about you. That, I promise."

"Not even Allison or Ken?" Steph glanced at her new friend. She and Allison had had a rocky relationship growing up, although Allison had invited her to lunch all those months ago.

"Allison? Nope. She said you were Drew's ex, and she covets your car, but nothing else. Ken? We don't talk except for polite conversation."

Dumbfounded, Steph said the only thing she could muster. "Huh."

Ciera turned around and looked out the plate glass window. "Where's your car?"

A jolt of fear snapped her out of that sense of wonder. "What? Oh, I sold it. Had to have some money to live on. I'm driving my dad's old truck."

"Boy, I can understand that. When we first came here, I counted every penny. Hollister is a good place to heal from things that have happened in the past."

Stephanie rolled her eyes. "Even if those bad things happened in Hollister?"

Ciera cocked her head. "I think it would be. If it happened here, healing here could give you a sense of closure I can't get from my past."

Ciera stood up and gently squeezed Stephanie's shoulder. "Let me know when you're ready, and I'll pull those chocolates out of the freezer.

Stephanie lifted her teacup and stared at the amber liquid. Zeke had flirted again. Did he mean the words? It wasn't an isolated incident. Could she let herself believe he wanted a relationship or maybe just a date? Lord, she prayed he didn't want a one-night stand.

She sighed and lowered the cup. The old wounds from Hollister were so minor compared to those inflicted in Colorado. She faced Ken and his attitude, but it had taken a lot to stand up for herself. Hell, she was still shaking from the encounter. Or was she shaking because of Zeke's words? Feeling a warm blush fan across her face, she dropped her gaze and stared at her meal. Was she ready for something? Was she ready for Zeke? Her heart whispered *yes*.

10

"Steph, it's damn near a blizzard. Are you sure you want to stay and do this?" Declan waved at the boxes of decorations strewn across the dancefloor. Her brother was closing early because no one was coming out with the threat of a major snowstorm pounding the area.

"Yep. I have the old four-wheel drive, and it won't take me long to get this done. An hour or so." She hoped. Looking at it, with all the pieces waiting to be put up, it might take a little longer. "If it gets too bad, I'll hunker down here."

"Declan, you ready?" Moe said from behind the bar.

"Yep, hold on a sec. Look, I got to run Moe home. His brother has the truck tonight. I'll come back and help." Her brother grabbed his jacket and put it on as he spoke.

"You'd have to pass the turn-off for home. I'll be done before you get back to town." She picked up a length of white fabric. "Now, go so I can get done." She pushed the ladder under the stud she wanted and stepped to the top of it. The first piece of fabric was stapled to the circular beam that held the elkhorn chandelier in the middle of the dancefloor.

"You leaving it like that?" Moe cocked his head and looked at the fall of fabric.

"No. I'm going to drape it to that wall, continue around this beam, and drape it out." She pointed as she spoke, showing Moe and her brother what she was doing.

"Going to look like a white big-top." Moe chuckled.

"That's the idea. Anything but a bar."

"Hey!" Declan lifted his arms. "It's a nice bar."

Stephanie chuffed as she descended the ladder. "It's still a bar. Now, would you two move, so I can finish?" She waved them off before moving the ladder around them to the far wall and picking up the fabric to staple into place.

"Fine, but you call me before you start home. I locked everything up and will throw the deadbolt when we leave. But you call me, hear?" Declan pointed to the wall phone.

"My hearing is excellent. I will call. Now, will you —please—go?" She snapped a staple into place with each pause.

"Going." Declan shook his head.

"You know, she's pretty feisty for a little slip of nothing." Moe chuckled as they walked out.

"Man, you don't have to tell me," Declan agreed.

Stephanie felt the blast of cold as the men left. *Finally*. She went to the old jukebox and flipped the switch behind it, allowing her to play music without paying. As an old Johnny Cash song filled the bar and an entire arm of old forty-five's queued into place, she pulled the next sheet of fabric off the stack and moved the ladder.

Five hours later, minus when Declan had called earlier in the night, she stood in the middle of the dancefloor and smiled. The Bit and Spur had been transformed into a winter fairyland. She'd hung clear plastic snowflakes that caught and refracted the fairy lights she'd strung throughout the bar. The silk and paper poinsettias and roses added just the right amount of color. The tables were draped, and the dancefloor was banked by tall tables with small bouquets of red silk and paper flowers.

She turned, giving every aspect a critical review. Well, until the power went out, that was. Steph groaned. "Great." The sudden loss of loud music in the background was eerie. It was pitch dark inside the windowless bar. With her hands out in front of her, she found her way to the bar and behind it, searching for the phone on the back wall by the liquor. She ran her hands lightly against the bar back, using the shelving as a guide. She noticed the howl of the wind from outside. The sound seemed to collide with the building. When she found the phone, she picked up the receiver and reached for the dial; only there was no dial tone. Stephanie clicked the button on the cradle. Nothing. Great. How long had the phone been out? Maybe that was why Declan had stopped calling? She glanced at the glow-in-the-dark dial of the now stopped clock that hung to the side of the bar. When had it gotten that late?

She fumbled her way to Declan's office and knocked over the lamp on his desk. "Damn it." Patting around until she found a clear space, which took a moment, she sat the lamp back up. The stacks of paper were unusual. Declan was a neat freak.

Stephanie knew he kept a flashlight in the top drawer. After a few moments of feeling through the pens and clutter, she finally found what she was looking for. A black metal flashlight flicked to life when her thumb slid the switch. The light was dim, but it was a light.

The top of the desk illuminated. Dang it. She'd made one hell of a mess. Setting down the light, she started to stack the papers, then stopped. She read the first paragraph, then the second. Her gut dropped to the floor, and she lost the ability to stand. She plopped down in Declan's chair and picked through the file that had spilled over his desk. No. No, no, no! Damn it, Declan, what were you doing? Reports and … Oh, God, pictures of Presley. The photos showed him going to work and entering the security gate at his house. There was a picture of him and another woman at dinner. No. She drew her hands through her curls. "What are you up to?" She reached for the phone again and prayed it would work. No dial tone. She sat back in the chair and stared at the file she'd shoved the documents into. The flashlight's glow dimmed again, pulling her attention from the file to her current situation. Stephanie dug through for a new pack of batteries. There wasn't any. Of course.

"Okay, Steph, time to go home." She was done anyway. She put on her coat, gloves, and snow boots before putting on her knit hat. The glow of the flashlight was getting weaker. Hopefully, it would hold until she got out of the pitch-dark bar. She swung the dull beam from the floor to the lower portion of the glass door. Snow banked against it. She lifted the light and froze. A silhouette of a man.

Screaming, she dropped the light. Then she dropped to her knees and scurried to find where the flashlight had rolled. She could use it as a weapon.

"Stephanie!" There was a pounding on the door. "Stephanie, are you all right?"

From her hands and knees, she looked up. "Zeke." She cleared her throat and yelled, "Zeke?"

"Yes, open the door." She stumbled forward and unbolted the door. Zeke and about three cubic feet of snow fell into the bar.

"Why are you here?" She shoved the door shut as fast as she could.

"Your brother asked me to come over. You didn't answer his calls, and he can't get here. His truck is high-centered near the end of the access road to your place. I said I'd come to see if you were still here. I didn't see a vehicle, so I didn't think you were here, but I needed to make sure."

"My truck is behind the bar."

"That's why I didn't see it. It's whiteout conditions out there. Power is out across town. You can't stay here, you don't have any heat source, and the weather people were way wrong. The storm is wicked and here a day early."

"I can't get home?" She clutched the keys to her dad's truck in her hand.

"Nope. I have room and plenty of firewood." Zeke grabbed her hand. "Come on, let's go before we're trapped here."

Stephanie knew the dangers of a blizzard. Staying at the bar without heat wasn't an option. "Are you sure? You know what people will think, right?"

Zeke stopped and closed the space between them. "I don't care what people think. I care about you. Now, come on, we need to go." He led her out of the bar and waited while she locked the door. As they cleared the small overhang sheltering the door, she was hit with the full force of the wind. They trudged to his truck that he'd left running, and he hoisted her into the passenger's side before getting in. He turned on the headlights, and she witnessed how bad the storm had gotten. "Wow."

"Yeah, it picked up steam over Wyoming, and it's dumping the frozen fields of hell on us now. You need to call Declan and tell him we're heading to my place to hunker down and wait for the storm to pass." He pointed to his cell phone. She dialed the number, and Declan answered on the first ring. "Did you find her?"

Stephanie answered, "Yes, I was at the bar. I didn't know it had gotten so bad."

"I freaking told you it was bad the last time we talked," Declan raged at her.

"You did." She closed her eyes. "I'm sorry. I had just a bit more to do. The phone is out, and the power went out just after I finished. I was on my way to Dad's truck when Zeke showed up." She glanced at her rescuer. His eyes were glued to the road, and the truck strained to plow through the snow even though it was a four-wheel drive and had chains on the tires. "Zeke said I could stay with him until the storm has passed."

"Good. Okay. Okay." Declan's anger appeared to be deflating.

"I didn't mean to worry you."

"Yeah, well, tell that to eight of my nine lives I lost tonight," Declan snipped back.

"I didn't hear it. The storm."

"How didn't you hear the wind howling?"

"Uh ... Johnny Cash, Waylon Jennings, Willie Nelson."

Declan chuckled. "Jamming out with the oldies."

"Guilty. I got the flashlight out of your office. You need new batteries. Oh, and that folder on top? That was interesting reading in there."

"Steph—"

"We'll talk about it when I get home." She wasn't going to let him go after Presley. Not that her ex didn't deserve Declan's wrath, but Declan didn't deserve the hell Presley's security detail would rain down on him.

"All right. I'm going to have a strong drink and hit the sack." Declan sighed. "I'm glad you're okay."

"Thank you for sending Zeke after me." She glanced again at her companion, who looked over at her and winked.

"Well, yeah. What else could I do? I'm stuck out here until the county can plow through the drift on the highway. The radio says the state transportation department has closed everything down, so it'll be a while before you can get here, or I can get there."

"Do you have enough food and firewood?"

"Yeah, I'm ok. You take care, okay?"

"I will. Night, Declan."

"Night, brat." He hung up before she could object to his childhood name for her.

"Hold on," Zeke said seconds after she hung up.

The truck tilted almost thirty degrees as it trundled through a drift she couldn't see. It took over ten minutes to get to his house on the other side of the small town. The weather stopped them several times because they couldn't see to move forward. Finally, he put the truck into Park on the side of his house, which blocked the wind. "Get inside. I need to plug the truck in before I come in."

"But the power is out."

"When it comes on, it'll defrost the block. Hopefully, I won't need the truck until the storm ends."

That made sense. Stephanie nodded and pushed her door open against the wind that, even while blocked, was still strong enough to press the door hard against her as she exited the truck.

She stood just inside his door and waited for him. His big frame brushed by her as he entered the house. "I have some candles. I'll light them and get the fire stoked." He took off his gloves and coat. "You can hang your outdoor clothes here. There's plenty of room." Zeke kicked off his cowboy boots and was gone a second later. She could hear him as she took off her coat, hat, and gloves. She pushed her hair out of her face and took off her shoes, lining up his boots and her shoes on the rug beside the door. Steph rubbed her arms and saw a glow illuminating the next room. She took a few steps forward and almost collided with Zeke. "Good, let's go in here. Shut the door behind you. We'll keep the area we heat to a minimum."

Stephanie closed the mudroom door and looked around the front room that opened into a nice kitchen. There was one hall off to the side where she assumed the bedrooms were. Zeke lit another candle and put the jar on a coffee table in front of a leather sofa. "Have a seat. I'll get this stoked." He grabbed a couple of smaller logs and crossed them over the coals in the fireplace. With the addition of a wad of paper under the smaller logs, the smoke billowed, and then, viola, flames. The fire licked at the loose bark of the aspen wood he'd put into the fireplace.

"I'm sorry you had to go out in the middle of the night."

Zeke chuckled and sat beside the fire, feeding it smaller kindling wood to keep the flames going. "I'm used to getting called out in the middle of the night."

Stephanie sat down on the couch. "Yes, but for emergencies. I was just ... stupid." She was also preoccupied with figuring out what in the hell had possessed Declan to spy on Presley.

Zeke's comment pulled her out of her, well, worry. "No, you got lost in your work. It happens.

Stupid would have been trying to drive home in this mess."

She shrugged. "I wouldn't have done that. I grew up in this weather." What would she have done, though? Tried to drive or walk to Ciera's or maybe Allison's? Probably. The Spur was on the outskirt of town just off the highway, and they would have been the closest people she knew. Thankfully, she didn't have to make that decision. "Anyway, I'm sorry I pulled you from your sleep."

"I wasn't sleeping. That family I told you about at the diner, the Thompsons, needed help. I'd just gotten home when Declan called."

"Is there anything I can do?"

He chuckled. "No. They were living in an RV that had no insulation. Mr. Marshall let them stay in one of the cottages." He nodded to the northeast. She knew immediately what cottages he was talking about. Nice places.

"Monty, his son Clay, and his father Chester were moving firewood along with another resident." Zeke grew quiet. "Monty slipped and took a fall on a patch of ice. He'll be fine, but when he hit, the skin on his forehead broke open. He never lost consciousness but needed stitches, and I gave him a couple of pain relievers."

Stephanie tucked her stocking-covered feet under her. "Are you supposed to be telling me this?"

Zeke chuckled. "You're going to be doing the paperwork for it. I don't figure we'll be dug out of this mess for at least a week. Talking shop, not gossiping."

She wrapped her arms around herself. "I'm sorry to intrude on your space."

Zeke looked up at her from his position in front of the fire. The golden light shadowed the features of his face. God, she so wasn't sorry. Being there with him felt safe, wonderful, almost magical. He smiled at her and turned back to feed the flames before he said, "I'm not."

11

Zeke rose to his knees and placed a sizeable slice of an old cottonwood tree onto the top of the flames. The storm howled outside, amplified by the absence of the HVAC system noises. He watched the flames feed on the fresh fuel with greedy licks.

"Are you flirting with me?" The soft question came from the corner of the couch Stephanie had tucked herself into.

He looked over his shoulder. Time to admit what he'd been dancing around. "God, I hope so. If not, I'm tragically inept. Maybe I should take lessons from Carson."

"God, no, please don't." She laughed a bit before moving her gaze from her fingers to the flames, completely avoiding eye contact with him. "I was in a bad relationship."

"They happen. Did it last long?" He didn't want to open closing wounds, but getting her to trust him with the truth would be a step in the right direction for them.

She snorted. "Far longer than it should have."

"I've worked in emergency rooms where some bad relationships end up. There's nothing to be embarrassed about. Corporate lawyers, doctors, and CEOs have all fallen victim to bad relationships. It isn't about love usually. It's about control."

Stephanie turned her gaze to him. "Control," she whispered the word, then nodded her head.

Zeke stood up and moved to sit at the opposite end of the couch. "But you're out now?"

"I am." She nodded again, her golden curls bouncing. "Completely. I hope." She sighed. "Declan has pictures of him. Reports from a private detective. I told him how bad it had gotten, and I think he wants to make my ex pay. What he doesn't understand is how dangerous Presley is."

Zeke almost choked, holding back his snort. "Presley?"

"Stop." Stephanie tried to rebuke him, but she smiled, too. *Yeah, Presley is a girl's name, isn't it?* Zeke stared at her until she looked at him. Her pain wasn't a joke, and he needed her to know he cared.

"Why would Declan have a file like that?"

"I think he's going to do something stupid like confront him. That would be a mistake. Presley is a dangerous man." She shivered and rubbed her arms.

"How bad was it?"

Stephanie held his gaze, and he could almost swear her eyes misted over, but it was hard to tell in the firelight. Finally, she spoke. "He was abusive, controlling, and I didn't see it at the time, but he isolated me from all my friends. He was so charming initially, everything that people here weren't. He wore suits and big flashy watches. Had personal trainers and was always surrounded by a security team. He convinced me I was his one and only. He made me believe my friends were jealous of us when they questioned him for preferring I not go out to do things with the girls. I let it go because I thought he was the one, you know? Only, when I finally understood what was happening, I had nowhere to go. He started to hit me. Then he would apologize and swear it would never happen again. He stopped apologizing. You can probably guess how bad it got."

Zeke closed his eyes. He didn't have to guess. He was in that changing room next to her when Declan found the cigarette burns on her back. "Why didn't you come back here?"

A sad laugh floated in the quiet to him. "Pride. God, that sounds pathetic, doesn't it? I left this place and vowed *never* to come back. I couldn't let the people who ran me out of town see how badly I'd failed at life." She wiped a tear from her eye and shook her head. "After a while, coming back was my best and only option."

Zeke grabbed the quilt from the back of the leather couch. He spread it out between them to stave off the sub-zero temperatures that had dramatically cooled the environment of the house without the heater working. He lifted his feet under it, and Stephanie moved under the blanket, too. Her feet reached his knees, and his legs extended almost to her corner of the couch, but they made room for each other and warmed up as the fire projected heat into the room. "Is there any chance this guy will come looking for you?"

Stephanie shook her head. "Honestly, I don't know. Declan doesn't think so." She looked up into his eyes. "Will this stop me from getting the job?"

Zeke pulled his eyebrows together in confusion. "Why would it?"

She sighed and stared at her hands again. "I don't know."

There wasn't any reason he could think of except … "Did you lie on your application?"

Her head snapped up. "No."

That was the only hurdle he could imagine that would invalidate her employment. "Then there's nothing to worry about. If he comes back, he'll have Declan to deal with and me, too."

She stared at him. "Why?"

"Because I'm flirting with you, remember."

"But why?" Stephanie's big blue eyes searched his face as if looking for an answer. He guessed he owed her his story after she'd told him hers. "Ever hear the saying unlucky in love?"

She snorted. "Yeah, I lived it." She cocked her head. "Doctor, do you need a hearing test?"

He chuckled. "No. I might not have had abusive relationships, but the ones I have had were, God, this is going to sound bad, but they were train-wrecks." He held up a hand. "Mostly my fault, I guess. I fell hard for someone many years ago, and she didn't feel the same way. She friend-zoned me."

Stephanie hissed and made a face. "Not the *friend* zone."

He laughed. "I can joke about it now. The man

she was interested in married her, and they're utterly happy and have a great family."

"Is she still in the local area?" Steph leaned forward. "You don't have to answer that. It was completely nosey. I'm sorry."

Zeke smiled at her. "Yeah, she is. Eden Wheeler."

Stephanie's eyes popped wide. "Your partner's wife?"

"We aren't actually partners. We have individual practices. The office building is his, and I rent out space. But yes, Jeremiah swept into town, and that was it for Eden. They fit together. I always knew it, just hated to admit it."

"Must have been hard to watch them together." Steph lowered her eyes. "But everyone deserves to find love. At least I thought they did." Stephanie slipped farther down and rested her head against the arm of the couch. Her toes rested midway up his thigh on a small sliver of the couch that his body didn't cover.

"I'd given up looking. I figured I'd be a bachelor for the rest of my life. Nobody quite measured up after her. Until now." He lifted one of her feet and rubbed the bottom of it through her sock. The delightful sound that rolled out of her slammed blood to parts of his body that he didn't want to let play into the conversation. Yet.

She spoke after a few moments, "I don't either. Measure up, that is."

He paused his massage, and she opened her eyes. "How do you know? You don't know what I'm measuring."

"True, but I'm pretty sure you're not seeing the real me."

Zeke switched feet and started to rub the other one. "What I see is a woman who truly cares about people."

Steph cocked her head as it rested on the arm of the couch. "That isn't a very high bar. Most people care about others."

Zeke continued to massage her foot. "Yes, but not in the way you do. You have next to nothing, yet you were willing to give your time and whatever you had to a family you didn't know."

"That's the way we were raised."

"Your mom and dad are gone?" As Zeke rubbed her foot, he could feel her relaxing under his touch.

She smiled sadly. "Yes. Our mom and dad were amazing people. They adopted Declan in their early fifties and me four years later. Declan and I have the same mother, different fathers, or so we were told.

Neither one of us has met our bio mom. We didn't want anything to do with her. We knew who our parents were. My dad died of a heart attack when I was a junior, and my mom passed a year later when I was a senior in high school. I think she died of a broken heart. She and Dad were part of the same soul. Declan stepped in as my guardian until I turned eighteen, and that was probably when he became my personal protector and crusader. You mentioned your mom. She lives in Florida?"

"She does. She married Pete in my first year of college. He's a great guy, and I call him Dad. She deserves the life and love he gives her."

"Your bio dad?" Steph asked.

"Never knew him. My mom was my only parent growing up."

"Where did you grow up?"

"Hot Springs."

"Really? A Black Hills boy?"

"All my life. I went to school and came back specifically to practice in a rural, underserved community." He loved the work. He'd never get rich doing it, but that wasn't why he'd gotten into medicine. Because he worked in an underserved community, the state paid his student loans, a benefit he hadn't expected.

"Having a doctor up here is a wonderful thing. There were so many times growing up when people had to race to Belle or Rapid. People died or lost limbs because of the time it took to get to the hospital. The community really needed one."

They sat quietly for a moment before Zeke spoke again. "I see how soft your heart is. I know how much you worry about the town's opinion of you. I know you like Gen and wish nothing but the best for her and Andrew."

"Did I tell you that?" She cocked her head.

"I watch and listen, Steph. I'm attracted to you, physically, yes, but I'm also attracted to the person who would spend the entire night decorating a bar for her ex-fiancé's new wife."

She shook her head, "It was the least I could do."

"My point." Zeke laughed when she rolled her eyes.

"So, what are you looking for between us?" The words were quiet, but he could tell the answer was important to her.

"I want to get to know you. I want to make out on this couch, but I'm also a forty-two-year-old man. I want more than a heavy make-out session, but I don't want to rush things. I don't want to push you into something you're not ready for. I'll wait." He'd have blue balls and probably jerk off three times a day, which was about twice more than his usual.

"You haven't even kissed me. What if we don't have chemistry?" She pulled her foot out of his hands.

He stared at her. "Let me kiss you."

She tucked her legs under her and crawled forward toward him, straddling him and placing her hands on his chest, never breaking eye contact. Her eyes flashed to his lips before she dipped down. He let her lead the kiss, and it was everything he could do not to roll her under him and devour her. She was sweet as honey. Her scent and taste sent his body into a head spin he didn't want to end. Her lips opened, and her tongue darted out, caressing his lips. He slid his hands up her waist, and she folded against him. Fuck, she was delicious and fit against him perfectly.

She ended the kiss and lifted away slowly. Her eyes were dilated when she licked her kiss-swollen lips. He croaked out, "Jesus, chemistry is not a problem."

She shook her head. "Definitely not. But maybe we should test it again, just to make sure?"

He slid his palm to her cheek and pulled her down, taking the lead. He needed her to know how much he wanted her, but he also needed to go slow with her. It was a feeling deep inside that told him not to force the physical side of the relationship.

He held her against him, careful not to make her feel trapped. A roll of his hips let her know how she affected him. He slowly lowered the passion and urgency of the kiss. Ending with several light kisses brushed against her slightly open lips. “You need sleep.” He smiled at her when she huffed out a sound of frustration.

“Sleep is not on my mind.” She dropped her head to his shoulder.

“Nor mine, but I don’t want to rush this, us. Sleeping here on the couch would be the warmest place in the house, but I’ll sleep in my room if you don’t want to share the couch.”

Steph moved. “Scooch.” He rolled onto his side and pushed back into the back of the couch, and she laid beside him, the small spoon to his larger frame. “I never thought the night would end this way.” She sighed and wiggled back against him.

Zeke about shot in his jeans like a hormone-raging thirteen-year-old. “Neither did I.” God, he hoped that didn’t sound as desperate as he felt.

“Goodnight, Zeke.” She settled beside him.

Bending forward, he kissed the top of her head. "Goodnight."

He watched the fire and listened to the crackling of the wood as it burned and the occasional popping of sap as the flame consumed it. Stephanie's breath evened out, and he managed to bring his body under control. Laying there with her, he felt content. A feeling he'd never been able to acquire in his other relationships. The "rightness" he was looking for had always been outside his grasp. Not so with Stephanie. That feeling of finding what he'd been searching for permeated the room and soaked through his skin, blood, and DNA.

12

Stephanie woke up with a start. The seconds it took to remember where she was and who she was with put years on her life. Finally able to draw a deep breath, she settled back onto Zeke's arm. Lord, her heart rate was pegged in the red zone. She drew another breath and tried to control the fear that had tackled her.

"You okay?"

Stephanie tipped her head up. Zeke's eyes were still closed. He had a morning scruff of dark blond hair on his face. She reached up and drew her fingers through the short stubby whiskers. "I'm okay. I didn't remember where I was."

Zeke kissed her finger as she ran it along his lips,

and she smiled and did it again. "You're with me. You're safe."

A contented sound escaped her as she let her hand fall to his chest. His muscles moved under her hand. The man was at least twice the size of Presley, but she didn't feel any fear. Instead, she felt protected. "What time is it?" she whispered.

"Last time I checked, it was almost ten."

Stephanie lifted onto her elbow and looked out the window. "It's still dark."

"The storm," Zeke said and opened his eyes. "Hungry?"

Stephanie turned her attention to the sexy man lying against her. "Yes." She was starving for affection and his touch, but she wasn't sure how to articulate her need, and she wasn't ready for sex yet, either. Or was she? Maybe. God, she didn't want to be a tease with her indecision.

He stared at her intently. "What?"

She opened her mouth, but the words didn't come out. "I ..." She shook her head and groaned.

He chuckled and pulled her in for a hug, and she rested against his chest. Zeke rubbed her back as he yawned. "No sense trying to think on an empty stomach. Stay under the covers until I get the fire going again." He flipped off the quilt, and she squeaked at the flood of cold air that splashed over her body's warm skin. He stood and stretched, his shirt lifted, and she saw his dark blond happy trail dive beneath his low-slung waistband. She blinked and snapped her gaze up to his face. He winked at her.

Mortified being caught eyeing him, she pulled the blanket over her head, causing him to laugh again. Steph peeked out of the blanket and watched as he restoked the fire. "I'll go heat some water so we can wash up."

"I can do that." She pushed the blanket off and shivered. "Do you have a sweater or maybe a sweat-shirt?" she asked, rubbing her arms. The cold was something she'd learned to live with. Still, layers were necessary when the power went out, and the fireplaces or old potbellied stoves were the only thing producing heat.

"No problem. The stove is gas. If you have any issues starting the burner, the matches are in the cabinet to the left. I'll be right back."

Stephanie made her way into the kitchen. The tile floor was cold, and her socks did little to stop the icy feel from assaulting her toes. The dark gray clouds seemed to settle over the little town, and snow still fell. Steph stood transfixed at the drifts that had blown in front of Zeke's truck. They were higher than the cab.

"Wow," he said as he came up behind her.

"Right?" She shook her head. "I haven't been in a storm this bad in a long time."

"My first year out here, there was one right after Christmas. It took weeks to get everything, and everyone dug out." Zeke placed something over her shoulders.

"Thank you." She shrugged into the wool-lined zip-up hoodie.

"I brought these for you, too." He handed her a pair of thick wool socks. "My feet always get cold."

"Perfect." She sat down at the small table and put on the socks. She pulled them all the way up to her knee, then pulled the tops down and over her feet again, doubling the thickness. "I'll get that water on now."

Zeke pulled out a large pan. "If you start the burner, I'll get the snow."

"Snow? Are the pipes frozen?" She reached for the matches.

"The ones in the bathroom are. Looks like we're melting water for the bathroom. I have plenty of bottled water stored in my workout room."

"Workout room?" She lit the range and watched as Zeke slipped into his boots and coat.

"I'll give you a tour." He winked at her and opened the door, quickly ducking out with the pan. She watched as he moved through the knee-deep snow and made it to the drift. He packed the snow into the pan and headed back. She was at the door and took it from him so he could dust the snow off his jeans. "It is not letting up out there." Zeke shook like a dog and sent snow in all directions in the mud room.

"I hope everyone is prepared. There always seems to be one family that has problems." She sat the pan on the burner and turned to look out of the window.

"Speaking of which … After we get something to eat, I'm going to go over to the Thompsons' and make sure they know how to get water and use it to flush the toilets and such if the pipes freeze up. I don't know how well insulated those cottage pipes are." Zeke reached for an oversized cable knit sweater hanging on a peg with the coats and put it on.

"Do they have enough food?" She remembered a couple of storms where they ran short at the old place. They couldn't get to the root cellar because it was buried under a ton of snow. Her mom had started keeping a closet to fill with root cellar items when they knew a storm was coming. You live and learn.

He nodded. "I made sure of it. Just didn't think to tell them how to melt the snow for the necessities."

"How far is it from here?" She couldn't see much of anything because of the blowing snow outside.

"About a quarter to a half mile in that direction." She gazed through the window in the direction he'd pointed. "Are you sure you can make it?"

"I'll be fine. It'll be my cardio for the day." He laughed. "I have eggs and bacon. We can toast the bread in the frypan."

"Let me cook. I mean, I'm imposing on you." She reached for the refrigerator's handle, but his arm on hers stopped her. He turned her toward him. "You are not imposing. I want you here, and call me selfish, but this time alone is time we can get to know one another better." He dropped his head and kissed her. She gasped and backed away.

"What?" He blinked, confused.

"I'm sorry, it's just that I haven't ... brushed my teeth, and I didn't want to ..."

His confusion turned into amusement. He

stalked toward her. "Neither have I. We cancel each other out. Just like garlic."

She stepped back, playing with him. "Is that so?" He took a step forward, and she retreated a step.

"Promise." He moved again. She bumped into the wall and waited for him. Then he placed his hands on her hips, and she wrapped hers around his neck, standing on her toes. "Don't promise unless you're prepared to keep it."

He leaned down and kissed her, and she sighed into the contact. So different, so right. When he lifted away, she kept her arms linked around his neck. "Did I keep my promise?"

She smiled up at him. "You did. A good way to start."

"An excellent way to start." He lowered for another kiss, and Stephanie lost track of time, of the storm, of the cold, of everything except for the man who seemed to surround her and encompass her in a feeling she'd never had the faith she would feel again. Need rushed through her, and her desire grew with each of his gentle and seductive touches. "Shit."

Zeke bolted to the range. The water from the melted snow was boiling. He turned off the water and looked back at her. "I guess we got distracted."

She pulled her shirt back down, remembering

the feel of his big hand against her breast. “Yeah, I guess we did.” She leaned back against the wall, unsure if her knees would hold her up. He walked back to her and caressed her cheek with two fingers. She leaned into his touch. “It’s been a long time since I wanted to be with someone.”

He nodded. “I know. But we’re going to make sure this, what’s building between us, isn’t something you’ll one day regret.”

Steph felt her brows crunch in confusion. “Why would I regret it?”

“I don’t want to be your rebound.” He winked at her and spun on his sock-footed heel. “Eggs and bacon?”

“Sure. Let me make it.” She hustled to the range and moved the hot snow water to the sink. “I’ll go get some more snow so we can use it to wash and flush the toilet.” He ducked down and opened a cupboard. Two empty one-gallon ice cream pails came back up with him.

“Do you like ice cream?” She looked pointedly at the containers.

“I do. I have a little bit every night in the summer. These work great for freezing trout and gathering snow. I have five or six under there.” He headed to the mud room.

"You know I got the better end of this deal, right? I don't have to go out in the cold," she quipped as she pulled an old coffee can out of the refrigerator. "Is this what I think it is?"

"Yep. Strained bacon grease," he said from the mud room where he was putting on his snow boots.

She sat it on the counter. "It makes great toast." Her mom used to put a thin layer in a cast iron skillet and toast their bread in it on Sunday mornings.

Zeke stood up and took off his sweater. She watched as the pull drew his t-shirt up to his neck, and it felt as if her eyes almost bulged out of their socket. But there was nothing she could do except stare at all the bare skin of his chest and stomach as he struggled to pull the sweater off. Damn, the man was built. Bulked heavy with muscle but in the best possible way. She cleared her throat and turned away before he caught her ogling him again.

"I only use it once a week. Everything in moderation." He grabbed his coat and elbowed into it.

She glanced at him. "Is that a thing? Moderation?"

He cocked his head and then laughed. "Not with you, it isn't." He winked at her again and headed outside with his buckets.

STEPHANIE TOSSED the last paper plate into the trash. She'd found Zeke's stash of disposable plates while he was washing up in the bathroom. It had been a long time since she'd poured water into the toilet tank so it could flush. About as long as it had been since she'd taken a sponge bath, but she'd grown up doing things like that, so it was second nature.

Zeke's cell phone chirped beside her. She glanced at the screen. A text from Phil Granger. She grabbed the phone and walked down the hall. "Zeke, you have a text from Phil." The bathroom door opened, and Zeke, sans shirt with a face full of shaving cream, peered out at her. "Read it for me, would you?" He lifted a straight-edged razor and turned back to the mirror.

Stephanie tore her eyes from his shoulders and back and called the text up. "Ummm ... 'The state police have closed all highways and anticipate they will stay closed for the next twenty-four to forty-eight hours'."

"We knew that." He took a long scrape down one cheek and dipped the razor into a small bowl he'd filled with water.

"That's a given. He said that he checked on the

families in the cabins. No water. He had extra and made sure they were okay. He said he took care of the Thompsons, so you don't need to go over."

"Good. I wasn't looking forward to playing in the snow."

The phone pinged again. "Mr. Marshall sent you a text."

Zeke frowned. "What does it say?"

"'Everything is okay out there. No need to check on them. They have power and will plow the road when the snow stops'."

"Good. That means I'm yours all day. Unless an emergency comes up." He scraped his cheek again.

"I was poking around in your freezer. We should set everything outside in a cooler, so it doesn't defrost."

"Good idea. I have some coolers stashed. I'll grab them." He bent over and splashed his face with water from the bowl.

Stephanie stared at him when he covered his face with the towel. His mountainous shoulders tapered into a narrow waist, and she wondered if he was big all over. *Dear Lord.* She turned and headed back to the kitchen.

"Hey, where are you going?" Zeke called from the bathroom.

"To, ah ... to do something out here," she called back. *Tea. You need a cup of tea.* She scrounged through the cupboards until she found his stash. She used the last water bottle and poured it into a small saucepan to warm up. "Do you want tea?"

"Yes, please." The call came from the back of the house. "Something warm sounds good."

"Yeah, it does." She said as she looked at the fridge. "Hey, should we make a stew?" she called back down the hall. "You have veggies."

"I have stew meat, but it's antelope. That all right with you?" Zeke said as he walked into the kitchen.

"Yep. Dutch oven?" She glanced around as she asked.

"Bottom cabinet by the oven."

"Perfect. I can make some hardtack, too." She'd made the fireplace bread since her mom taught her when she was ... gosh ... maybe six.

"Hardtack?" He chuckled and pulled out vegetables from the fridge and two packs of antelope stew meat from the freezer.

"It's what we called it. It's bread, a normal recipe, punched down in a round circle. You can bake it in a skillet over the fire. We used a weighted down sheet pan as the cover."

"How do you get it to rise?" He pulled out the Dutch oven and placed it on the counter.

"That's the fun part. You have to sit by the fire and rotate the bowl. Declan and I would play cards, and between each hand, we'd turn the bowl a half rotation, keeping it warm enough to rise a bit. It doesn't get as high as normal bread, but when you cook it, it has a deep yeasty flavor."

"Sounds delicious. What do you need me to do?" Zeke put his hands on his hips.

"The food in the fridge first. It needs to go outside where it won't defrost."

"On it."

Stephanie pulled out the bacon grease and dolloped a couple of spoonfuls into the Dutch oven's bottom before Zeke took the grease outside. She placed the antelope meat on a paper plate and took it into the living room, sitting it beside the fire to defrost.

Within minutes, she'd poured hot water for their tea, mixed together the bread dough, and was kneading it by the time Zeke had finished clearing out the refrigerator and freezer. She placed a dish-cloth down on the hearth, then the bowl with the bread dough, and covered it with another cloth.

"Is the antelope defrosted?"

"I think we can break it apart." She manipulated the package it was in. "We need to cook this meat for a long time, or it will be tougher than an old goat."

"Don't I know it? The first time I tried to make anything out of antelope, it was as if I was chewing a rubber tire." Zeke laughed. "I don't hunt, but patients bring stuff by all the time. I figured you treat it the same way you treat venison."

Steph chuckled. "Nope. Not even close, although both are lean, antelope is a stringy critter, as my mom would say. You cut it always against the grain, and if you're stewing it, you let it go for hours. Work on breaking these frozen pieces up, would you?" She handed him the meat, and they worked together to brown it with a generous dusting of flour and spices. Once all the pieces were dark brown and completely seared, she added a bottle of water, which Zeke had resupplied when he finished emptying the fridge. She dashed in more spices and stirred, scraping the brown bits off the bottom of the pan. Then she put the lid on. "In the coals." She nodded to the living room.

"We have gas." Zeke pointed to the stove where she'd browned the meat.

Stephanie stopped as a shard of fear that she was messing up jumped into her heart. No. No, Zeke wasn't Presley. He wasn't mad at her. She drew a breath and let it out. She was safe there. Protected. She shook her head. "This is better. Trust me." She loved cooking in the fireplace. It was a snowstorm tradition. One that she didn't realize how much she'd missed.

Zeke snorted. "I will defer to your better judgment." He helped her in the kitchen and carried the heavy pot to the fireplace.

"What now?" Zeke asked after they settled the Dutch oven into the coals and bank some around the sides.

"Now we play cards." She dusted her hands off. "Where are they?"

"I don't have any." Zeke rubbed his chin. "But I do have something. I'll be right back." Stephanie pushed the coffee table nearer to the fire. She tossed down the seat cushions from the two wingback chairs situated on either side of the couch. One for him and one for her.

Zeke came back in with an ancient-looking tin. "Dominos."

He opened the tin, and she gasped. "They look like ivory."

"I think they are. Wallace Lamont gave them to me when he was first diagnosed with stage four cancer. He said he wanted to give me these while he was still of his own mind. They were his grandfather's."

"Do you know how to play?" she asked him as they carefully took out the rectangle tiles.

"I do. That's why Wallace gave them to me. I bested him sometimes, but he usually schooled me." Zeke shook his head. "I'm going to miss that guy."

"He was a feature in this town forever. I liked him." Steph mourned the loss of someone so prominent in Hollister's community. Wallace was known by everyone. She moved the old tin and smiled up at Zeke. "So show me how you play."

13

Zeke leaned back against the couch. “Oh, that was good.” He’d been smelling the cooking stew all day and had eaten half the bread Steph had made ... before dinner.

“Mom said the fireplace stew always tasted better because of the all-day aroma.” Steph popped the last of her small piece of bread into her mouth and leaned back next to him.

He dropped his arm over her shoulder, and she nestled into his side. “You snookered me. You’re a domino pro.”

“I didn’t!” She laughed at him. “I asked you to show me how *you* play. Different people have different rules.” Dominos and cards were a staple when they were snowed in or when the television reception was horrible, which was quite often.

"I'm not buying it. It was a set-up." Zeke pulled her closer. "This has been the best snow day of my life."

"It has been wonderful." She sighed and pointed at the dishes. "They aren't going to clean themselves."

He grunted. They probably wouldn't, but he wasn't in the mood to move, and by her lack of action, she probably wasn't either. "They'll wait."

"Oh." She chuckled. "Good to know." She moved anyway, and he lifted his arm. Instead of moving toward the coffee table, she straddled him and sat on his lap. He caught her mischievous smile before she dropped her head for a kiss. His hands found her waist under the fleece-lined hoodie she'd worn all day and moved beyond. He filled his hand with her breast and thumbed the nipple. She moaned into his mouth and pushed closer. Fuck, he wanted to make love to her, but ..."

He broke the kiss. "The dishes."

"Screw the dishes." Stephanie dropped down and tried to kiss him again.

He pushed back away from her lips, stopping her advancement. Quickly, he explained, "If we start this again, it would be challenging for me to stop." Not that he *wouldn't* stop. He'd fucking cut off his dick rather than do anything she didn't want to do. Stephanie had lived through a relationship of non-consent and brutality. He wanted her to know where he was far enough in advance to put the brakes on.

She sat back, and his eyes rolled into his head when her slight weight put pressure on his hard-as-a-diamond cock. He'd had a semi-hard on all day, and yes, he'd reverted to a thirteen-year-old, but damn it, Stephanie did it for him. Even wrapped in a hoodie five sizes too big, with rolled-up sleeves and socks doubled over, the woman called to him like a siren. He was lost at sea when it came to her. He'd follow her song, and damn, he prayed the object of his desire felt the same way about him.

"What if I don't want to stop at kissing? What if I want to see you, all of you." She ran her hands up his shoulders while staring at him.

"I'd want to see you and touch you." His hands were still on her waist, and he held them there, not wanting to sway her answer.

"I won't be a one-and-done. That's not me, contrary to what this town believes." She lowered her eyes. "If we follow the feelings we're experiencing, I'd be the only one you're with." She jerked her head up. "God, that sounded wrong. I don't want to control you. I never want that to happen. It's just—"

Zeke sat up, which nearly strangled his dick, but the woman on his lap was spinning, and he needed to stop her before she crashed. "Hey, you have every right to have expectations in this relationship. We both do. If I'm with you, I'm only with you. That isn't demanding. It's a matter of trust and commitment.

"It's hard for me." She snorted and dropped her head to his chest. "For you, too, obviously." She wiggled just a bit, and he groaned.

"I want you, Steph. There's no denying it. The spark started at the clinic that night when you came in looking like a drenched kitten and farted on my exam table."

"What!" She sat up, her eyes as big as saucers. "I didn't!"

He laughed and dodged a half-hearted swipe with her hand, catching her hands in one of his. "Sorry, sorry. I couldn't resist."

"My clothes stuck to the table." She grumped the words and dropped against his chest.

"I know. But it's a great story."

"It isn't." She shook her head. "It really isn't."

He wrapped her in his arms. "I'd like to be with you, Steph. I've told you that. When that happens is absolutely up to you. I'm not looking for anything with anyone else, so I'll wait as long as necessary. I'd honestly given up and was ready to live my life as a crotchety old bachelor."

She lifted so she could see him. "What changed your mind."

He shrugged. "A fart."

"Oh, gawd!" She groaned and flopped to the side. He followed her, placing her under him. All the laughter died as their eyes connected, and she lifted her hand to his cheek. "Just us."

"You have my oath."

"Oath?" She ran her fingers along the bottom of his lower lip.

"An oath, a pledge of my sincerity given to you." He kissed her fingertips.

"Don't change, Zeke. Don't ever change." It was a plea. That bastard had changed, tricked, and trapped her.

"You've seen the real me, Steph. There's nothing more, nothing less." He dropped and kissed her. Her legs moved and cradled him as they adjusted their positions, not breaking a kiss that seemed more important than air. Eventually, he had to lift. As she panted under him, he followed the ridge of her jaw to her neck, then lower to her collarbone. She pushed on him, and when he lifted, she unzipped the hoodie and flopped out of the arms.

Zeke found her flat stomach and pushed up her shirt, finding the lace of her bra. He lowered his mouth, and after releasing her breasts from the barely-there material, he suckled each nipple to a hard pebble. Her hands pushed, demanding he remove his sweater. As much as he didn't want to move, he lifted and tore off the sweater and t-shirt under it in one go. As he started to move back down, she put her hand on his chest. "All of it." She looked at him through hooded eyes. Her kiss-swollen lips, partially open and glistening, fascinated him. God, the woman was beautiful.

She pushed his chest again. "Clothes." He stood up and unfastened the large silver buckle on his belt as Stephanie sat up and removed her shirt. He once again lost track of what he was doing as she unzipped her jeans and wiggled out of them, revealing miles of skin.

"You're beautiful."

She shook her head. "I'm not, but I'm getting cold."

Zeke flashed into action, grabbing the quilt from the back of the couch and dropping it to the floor beside her. Then he unzipped and removed his jeans, shedding his socks with them. He went to the floor and crawled over her, his briefs still in place. He'd take it at her pace. When he was over her, he flung the quilt over his back. "Better?"

She smiled. "Much." Her arms wrapped around his neck, and he lowered, giving her some of his weight. Their tongues danced, and their hands explored. Breaking the kiss, he once again moved down her body, giving her breasts a teasing kiss and flick of his tongue before moving lower. He swirled his tongue across her hip bone, nipping the soft skin before he wet it again with his tongue and blew across the damp skin. She shuddered under his hands. He lifted his head, and the vision of her on her elbows watching him sent a white-hot jolt to his cock. He lowered farther, kissing his way to her core.

As he moved, he slid his shoulders under her thighs and pulled the little piece of lace out of his way. His first taste of her exploded across his senses. Fuck, yes. He opened her with his fingers and made it his mission to make her scream with pleasure. Her hand gripped the hair on the top of his head, and he doubled his efforts as her hips thrust up to meet his mouth. He glanced up at her body and saw her hand on her breast, pulling gently on the nipple. He groaned at the erotic vision, and her hips thrust again, harder. He pinned her to the floor with his arms wrapped around her thighs and feasted. She tightened under him, her thighs trembling. God, yes. He'd die a happy man if he could make her come from—

Stephanie's body erupted and drenched him in her juices, glazing his face. Fuck, every damn erotic thought he'd ever had, coalesced in her. He waited until she stopped thrashing before he kissed his way back up her extremely sensitive expanse of skin. By the time he took her mouth, his cock had pushed the waistband of his briefs out of the way. Her hand reached down and circled his shaft. "Please." She stroked him through his briefs, and stars exploded behind his eyelids.

He dropped his head to her shoulder. "Condoms."

"I have an IUD." She ran her hands through his hair. As a doctor, it wasn't just an unwanted pregnancy about which he was concerned. He lifted his head, prepared to explain.

"I had tests done at the free clinic in Cheyenne on the way home. He didn't give me anything." She pulled him down. "Make me feel beautiful."

He lifted and tugged down his briefs, releasing his cock. "You are beautiful. You don't need anyone to make you feel that way. You are beautiful and so much more." He entered her as they shared a breath and kissed her when she gasped. He worked into her core and feasted on the essence of the woman under him. He changed angles, found several positions that drove her to mewling sounds, and committed each to memory. His fingers found the three burns on her back. She shook her head when he paused and looked down at her. No problem, he understood she didn't want that bastard there, not then. He continued to map her body with his hands. Her nails raked his back and her hips thrust up. "Yes," she panted the word, and with laser focus, he pushed her until she tightened around his shaft. Two strokes later, he lost himself inside her.

Collapsing to his elbows above her, he caught his breath. Her hands roamed his shoulders, and he lifted his head. Shit. Tears. "Did I hurt you?"

She shook her head and sniffed. "No. It isn't that."

He pulled out of her and laid beside her, pulling her into his embrace and flinging the quilt over them. "What is it?"

"That is the first time in years that I've come. That I've felt anything like this. It was beautiful."

She swiped at her cheeks. "Now you think I'm weird."

He chuckled. "Nah, this isn't weird. Farting on the exam table is weird." Her sob of laughter turned into tears. He held her, not knowing what else to do. Crap, he hoped he didn't screw it up. He kept her in his arms and stroked her hair until she stopped crying. "Better?"

She nodded. "I'm sorry."

"For what?" He kissed her forehead but didn't make her look at him. He had a feeling she was still working through whatever had made her cry. "I guess I needed to let it all go. The feelings and the fears."

"You never need to be afraid of me, Steph." That was a fact anyone could etch into stone.

"I know," she whispered. "It's hard to acknowledge all the bad things, so I can accept the good."

"Take your time, sweetheart. I'm not going anywhere." Zeke pulled her closer and waited as she snuggled into a comfortable position. She fell asleep next to him, wrapped in his arms as he promised the universe he'd make sure no one ever hurt her again.

14

Stephanie stood at the kitchen window and stared at the brilliant blue skies. The storm had moved east, and the cold, crisp air settled into a soft breeze. People would be out, digging their roadways, homes, and vehicles out of the snow. It would take longer for the state to open the highways and the counties to clear the secondary roads. She had another day, maybe two, with Zeke.

She listened to him whistle in the bathroom as he shaved. A smile spread across her face. They'd woken during the night and made love again. And again, that morning. She felt her cheeks heat. Every time, he made her melt. What she'd missed for all those years. No. Absolutely not. She wouldn't let her past interfere with her time with Zeke. It had erupted last night, and maybe the breakdown was a cleansing she needed because it was a new day. A new day without the shadow of Presley dimming her vision.

Zeke stopped behind her. “Looks like a nice day.”

“If nice is twenty-below.” She pointed at the thermometer hanging outside his kitchen window.

“Okay, rephrasing that. It looks like a clear day.” Zeke spun her and kissed her. She hung on, breathless, by the time he lifted away.

“What you do to me, doctor.” She sighed and leaned into him.

“That good, huh?” He grabbed her butt with both hands and hoisted her up his big body. She laughed and wrapped her arms around his neck. “What do you think you’re doing?”

“Kissing you.” He captured her lips and kissed her again.

She broke away to breathe. “You’re dangerous, Doctor Johnson.”

“No, ma’am. I’m your safe harbor in any storm.” Zeke stared at her. “You and me.”

She nodded. “You and me.”

A knock on the door spun him, which spun her. She twisted in his arms. “Let me down.”

"Why?" He walked to the door, still holding her, and opened it.

Phil Granger cocked his head. "Well, hello. Doc, Steph. I'm going to plow your driveway and get you a path to the clinic. The big trucks from the county won't be here for days."

"Put me down." Steph tapped his shoulder. Zeke made a face but let her down. "Phil, would you like some tea or cocoa?" she asked.

"No, thank you, Stephanie. I have my thermos, and I'm set. Just wanted Doc to know he could make it to the clinic. It'll be a walking path. There's too much snow for my small plow."

"Thank you, Phil. I appreciate the assistance."

"No worries. I hear the substation blew, which is why our power is down. According to the radio out of Belle, there are record outages, and Black Hills Power and Light are calling in people from other states to help restore it. Could be a week or more before we get completely dug out and power restored."

"We're set here." Zeke nodded.

"Do you know of anyone that needs anything, Phil? Anything I can do to help?" Stephanie asked.

"I don't, but I've just started getting around. If

there's something, I'll let you know. Thank you for offering."

"It's the least I can do. We're in this together." She said the exact words she'd heard her father say over and over again.

Phil smiled. "That's the truth, now, isn't it? I'll be getting after it now. Have a good day." Phil lifted a hand and stepped out of the mud room into the freezing weather.

"Well, everyone will know now." Stephanie shut the door and looked up at Zeke.

"I don't care." He shrugged. "Do you?"

Steph found herself smiling. "Not in the slightest."

"Good. Now, how about a rematch? I need to even the score." Zeke grabbed her hand and pulled her into the warm living room. The fire he'd stoked that morning was burning well.

"Okay, I'll play, but you can't pout when you lose." She emptied the tiles out of the tin and shuffled them by mixing them on the table. Then they drew their tiles.

"What's your favorite food?" she asked as she placed the double six tile.

His face screwed up, and his eyes scanned his tiles. "You stacked the tiles."

She laughed. "Impossible to do. Draw and answer my question."

"Fine." He drew until he could play. "Before yesterday, I'd say my mother's chicken and rice casserole. Now, campfire stew. Hands down. You?"

"Anything with a potato in it." She laughed when he looked up at her in question. "Seriously, I've never met a potato I didn't like. What's your least favorite food?"

He placed a tile after she did. "Mushrooms. Fungus is not meant to be consumed."

"I'll agree with you on that one." She drew three tiles before she was able to play. "What's your least favorite holiday?" She looked over at him.

"The fourth of July," he said quickly.

"Why? You have something against celebrating independence?"

"Not at all. I'm very pro-America, but I haven't had one go by without a major incident. Bar fights, injuries from the rodeo, car accidents, fireworks blowing up in someone's hand, you name it. People get hurt on the fourth, and that's why I'm not a fan."

She'd never thought about it that way, but she could see his point.

"What's your least favorite color?" he asked, continuing her questioning trend of least favorites.

"Orange."

He lifted his gaze from his tiles. "Why?"

"I was six, maybe seven, and my mom bought me this orange dress. I loved it, but it had all these, I don't know, like layers under the skirt that made it stick out like a hoop skirt. I wore it to church, and all the boys and girls called me pumpkin. It was my nickname for years. I never wore orange after that. If I ever do, you know something is seriously wrong."

He shook his head. "Okay, no orange."

"What about you?" she asked, placing another tile.

"I like all the colors. Don't have a favorite or a least favorite." He shrugged. "I'm weird that way."

"Not weird at all. I don't really have a favorite either." She watched him place another tile and then drew one, placing it on the end of the line.

"Least favorite football team?" She'd noticed several NFL magazines in a stack by the couch.

"I can't answer that." He shook his head.

"Why not?" She placed a tile and waited for him to move.

He didn't look at his tiles. "Because each team has strengths and weaknesses, the dynamics change yearly. I enjoy football for the sport, both college and professional. What team is playing isn't really relevant. *How* they play is the reason I watch."

"Rut-roh Scooby, we have a serious football fan on our hands." She laughed when he nodded solemnly. "Well, I watch football to cheer for the underdog."

"Why the underdog?"

"Because they need support." The duh at the end of the statement was implied.

"You really do have a kind heart." He smiled at her.

"Maybe." She waved at his tiles. "Your play."

He put down a tile and then asked. "Least favorite season?"

"Before yesterday, winter. Now, I'm kinda liking it,"

"Ditto." He chuckled.

"Hobbies?" she asked.

"Least favorite?" He made a face.

"No, do you have any?" She laughed when his confusion cleared up.

"I do. Weightlifting." He motioned to the other side of the house. "I built an addition to the house, and I have my weights and a few cardio machines in there. And I guess building the house is a hobby. I've got plans for a garage."

"Declan loves to build, and so did our father. Me, not so much, but I know how to use hand and power tools."

"What about you? Hobbies?"

She shook her head. "I haven't had the opportunity. But maybe I'll find something now." She tried not to let the reality of that statement bring the conversation down.

"Winter around here almost demands a hobby of some sort. Something will catch your attention." He pointed at her tiles, obviously catching on to the fact that she didn't want to linger on the topic.

She placed one, then asked, "What's your idea of a dream date?"

"Last night?" He looked at her, and she melted under the heat in his eyes. She'd never felt so cared for, so protected, and so safe. Zeke had wrapped her in his safety and carried her when she didn't know if she could walk in his direction.

"Yeah, that was amazing." She stared at him and forgot about the domino tiles when he lifted himself over the table and kissed her hard. The tiles scattered, but she didn't care. He moved around the table as he kissed her. The kiss consumed her mind, leaving her body and desires in charge. The clothes they'd put on earlier were cast off and scattered around where they lay, tangled together. She rolled him and glanced at the windows to make sure the drapes were drawn before she straddled him. She held his shaft and slowly lowered onto him. The angle was just different enough to make her shiver as her nerves adapted to the sensation of him filling her. His cock deep inside her twitched before she lifted off him. His hands found her breasts, and he played with her nipples. She threw back her head. Intense pleasure swamped her under a thousand sensations that rippled, ebbed, and flowed over her senses like a building tide. She shattered and dropped forward. Zeke caught her and found enough leverage to slam into her with rapid thrusts. He growled through his orgasm, finally stilling under her.

He rolled her and once again tossed the quilt over them. She lifted a finger, and when she could breathe, she waved at him. "Don't think I don't know you started this to get out of losing another domino game."

His laughter was contagious. She rolled into his embrace. *Thank you, God. Thank you for this man.*

15

Zeke grabbed Steph's hand as they walked over a large drift. The snow had iced over, and his weight broke through the crust.

"Are you sure you want me there?" She looked up at him, worried again.

"I am. Today is the first. You're an employee now. I'll get you into the database, and you can fill out the information after I see the patient while I'm making my notes. You have your own office and computer."

"I do?" She glanced up at him. A smile as bright as the South Dakota sun beamed up at him.

"You do. The first office closest to the entrance, so you'll hear people coming in."

"Is it busy, I mean, every day?"

"Not the office, necessarily, but with call-outs and my work for Guardian, I stay busy."

"Guardian?"

"A security company that has a presence in the area. They're paying part of your salary. My work for them is infrequent, but I enjoy it."

"Oh, Declan told me about them. They're the ones we don't talk about with strangers. I don't know why people need to stick their noses into things that don't concern them. Good people, by all accounts, right? Oh, shoot." She stopped. "Hold on. My shoe came off." She lifted her sock-clad foot. With fantastic balance, she reached down while holding her leg up and grabbed her shoe out of about ten inches of snow. She turned it over, and a deposit of snow fell into the hole that she'd pulled it out of. "Well, this is awkward."

Zeke laughed, and he knew why. Stephanie had a way of making him feel happy. Her good-natured personality, soft heart, and inner beauty made her physical attractiveness all the more vibrant. "Here, piggyback ride to the office." He turned and bent down.

"People are going to talk." She warned as she grabbed him around his neck, her empty shoe in one hand.

"They'll talk no matter what we do." He stood while bouncing her onto his back. "The people associated with Guardian are exceptional people."

"Who's waiting for us at the clinic?"

"Two patients. A hand from the Hollisters' ranch. They're coming in by snowmobile because the roads aren't cleared yet. The other is a Guardian. Has a sliver in his hand that he can't get out." According to the text from Mr. Marshall, the man would wait until Zeke could make his way to the clinic when the roads opened if needed. Since he was going in to see one of the Hollisters' hands who'd stayed out too long working in the weather, Zeke asked Mr. Marshall to relay he was on his way to the clinic and to have the Guardian meet him there.

"A sliver?" Steph leaned forward. "Not a very tough security dude, is he?"

"Now, now, Ms. Howard. We don't judge our patients." He hefted her up on his back. "At least not until we're home and no one else can hear us."

She laughed a bit. "That was wrong of me, wasn't it? I'm sorry."

"You can say anything to me, Steph. I'm not reprimanding you." He turned to see her as she peeked over his shoulder.

"I know. I just wouldn't want someone to talk about

me like that. I won't do it again." She dropped her chin onto his shoulder. "There are snowmobiles at the clinic." She pointed with the hand holding the shoe. Four figures stood outside the front door. Quite the crowd.

It took another minute to trudge through the snow to the office. Gen turned when he got closer. "Hey, I want a piggyback ride." She looked at Andrew but pointed at Zeke. "That looks like fun."

Andrew laughed and dropped his arm over his new bride. "For who? Hey, Steph, are you hitchhiking?"

"Kinda." She held up her shoe. "I had a blowout."

"Not fun." Gen shivered exaggeratedly.

"Okay, one-footed landing," Zeke told her as he slid her off his back. "Let me get the office open. Andrew, could you go to the back and crank up the generator?"

"The small outbuilding?" Andrew asked as he walked away.

"Yep." Zeke opened the door, and Gen helped Stephanie hop inside. "Okay, guys, come in." Zeke nodded at Rusty, who had his hand wrapped in about a thousand layers of fabric and taped into place as he walked in. Then he turned to the stranger, introducing himself, "I'm Doc Johnson. I understand you have a sliver?"

The man shook his head. "M-more l-like a l-og." He held up his hand, and Zeke adjusted his priorities immediately. The man had bandaged his hand, but he could see a thick portion of a branch had punctured it, and a shard was protruding out the other side.

"That should have been a stat call, not a when you can get to the office type of call." He motioned the man into the office.

"Rusty, exam room one. Gen, get his hand unwrapped. I need you not to move his fingers or brush anything against them."

"Yeah, we taped a bowl over them, so nothing would touch them. That's why he looks like he's swinging a caveman's club."

"Good on you. You can come with me." The man followed him back to his procedure room. "Go ahead and sit up there." The sound of the gasoline-powered generator came from the back of the building. "Okay, I'm going to get this unwrapped."

"Zeke, can I do anything to help?" He turned to see Stephanie, sans any shoes, standing at the door. "Yes. Turn on the light for me. While I wash up, pull a tray from the second shelf of that cabinet. Don't open it. It's sterile."

"The big one or the small one?" Stephanie asked as he scrubbed his hands. "The large one. Put it on that silver stand and wheel it to the exam table."

He wiped his hands and slid into gloves. "Okay, let's take a look at this." He started to unwrap the branch that had impaled the man. "What's your name?"

"S-Sage B-Browning."

Zeke looked up at him to assess his patient. "How long have you been out in the cold?"

"N-not the cold. Stutter." The man looked away quickly.

"Got it. New and tense environments make it worse, I assume." Sage nodded his head. "Okay, I'm going to be straight up with you. That little generator won't power my X-ray machine, but this needs to be removed. I'm going to numb your hand and do my best to get everything out. You're lucky it pierced the fleshy part of your hand."

Sage snorted. "R-right. That's m-me, Mr. L-Lucky."

Zeke smiled. The guy had a sarcastic comeback, but that piece of wood had to hurt like a bitch.

"Steph, I'm going to numb this before I look at

Rusty. Could you let them know I'll be there shortly?"

"You got it." She padded out of the room, and he went to work, numbing the area as well as he could. "I'm going to let that work and check on my other patient."

Sage nodded, and he made tracks for the exam room. After he washed his hands and re-gloved, he carefully removed the bowl protecting Rusty's hand.

"Yeah, you look like you got bit pretty good here and here." He gazed at the tips of the man's middle and ring finger of his left hand. "Are you right-handed?"

Rusty nodded. "It was cold, Doc, but I didn't think it was that cold. I was wearing leather gloves. The fingers went numb, but hell, that happens all the time. I went to the main house when I saw they'd turned gray and weren't getting pink. Senior made sure I kept them separate and didn't rub them. Gen fashioned this contraption, so I could get here on the snowmobile. Man, I feel like a darn fool." Rusty looked a little pale as he spoke. "Am I going to lose them?"

"You may have lucked out. This happened two days ago?" He examined the skin carefully. The skin was red and swollen. Small white blisters with clear fluid had formed, which was good. “Yeah, the day the storm hit. I just didn’t think it was that cold.”

“Well, we’ll have to monitor this to make sure it heals properly. But it looks like you have stage two frostbite. This area will probably turn redder, and your skin will peel like a sunburn. It may also ache, burn, or have needle-like sensations. And I’m not going to pull any punches here. You will be more susceptible to frostbite in the future. Leather work gloves won’t be enough to keep this from happening again.”

“I got you, Doc. I’ll wear the thermal ones. And it already aches.” Rusty nodded quickly.

“Over-the-counter pain pills. Make sure you don’t exceed the recommended dosage. I’ll wrap each of these individually. Gen, you’re doing the upkeep, right?” He looked over his shoulder at the newly minted Mrs. Hollister.

“You know it. I’ll make sure he behaves.” Gen nodded. Andrew crossed his arms and leaned back against the wall. “You did it now, Rusty. She’s going to go all mother hen on you.”

“I don’t mean to put no one out,” Rusty said in a hurried rush of words.

“You’re not.” Zeke, Gen, and Andrew replied at the same time.

Zeke chuckled. "See, it's unanimous. I have a brochure for exactly what to look for, and I'll give it to you before you leave. I'll need to see you again if you see blisters with blood in them or any blackness forming."

"Got it, Doc. Thanks." Rusty dipped his head again.

"No problem. I'm glad it wasn't more severe, and you did the right thing by getting it looked at." Zeke carefully wrapped each finger individually while showing Gen how he protected Rusty's fingers. "I'd still wrap that in that blanket on the way home. Don't go out in the cold without adequate protection."

"I'll make sure of it," Rusty acknowledged.

"Good, now give me a minute, and then Steph will come to get you to take care of the paperwork."

"Stephanie is working here?" Andrew asked.

"Sure is. Her first day is today," he said as he walked to Stephanie in her office to help her get set up. "Okay, here's the password."

He said the alphanumeric combination as he typed. She nodded. "Got it."

Zeke scrolled the mouse over an icon. "This is the billing software, but since we have no internet ..." Zeke clicked on the patient intake form. "This has all the information you'll need. I'll give you the rest after I see the patient. Usually, this portion should be filled out before the patient gets to me. It never works that way. Maybe you can make it happen. I'll be in the procedure room if you need me. Rusty is waiting for you to call him in."

"I've got it. Go do your sliver-ectomy."

Zeke chuckled and headed back to where he'd left Sage. Zeke cleaned up and dragged his stool over with his foot before he made sure the numbing agent had done its job. "Feel anything?"

"Other t-than stupid? Nope." Sage gave a small chuckle.

"How did it happen?"

"The b-boy in the n-next cabin went out f-for f-firewood. He d-didn't come b-back. Got ... l-lost."

"Who? Clay Thompson?"

Sage nodded his head. "F-found him. H-he g-got turned around. I t-tripped over the b-biggest part of this. It was b-buried."

"Why the hell was Clay out getting firewood? I'm sure there was enough." Zeke muttered to himself as he draped the area.

"Doc, sometimes it's n-not easy being y-young. He's a g-good k-kid. Needed space." Sage's words brought his eyes up. Something in the man's expression led him to believe Sage had personal experience with what he was talking about.

"Clay's a great kid from what I know about him. He's new to the area." Zeke went to work on the chunk of wood in the man's hand. He managed to remove it and spent more time making sure there was nothing left in Sage's hand that could fester. He placed ten internal stitches and then closed the external portion of the injury. He dressed the wound and sat back. "This is probably going to throb like hell. I can give you some low-dose prescription painkillers."

Sage shook his head. "No, t-thank you."

"All right, I can respect that. Over-the-counter pain relievers as needed. Any redness or swelling, you come back in. We should be open for business in a couple of days. It usually takes four or five days for everyone to return to normal after a storm like this. But if this gets infected, you call me." Zeke reached over to the small side desk and grabbed one of his cards with his cell phone number.

Sage nodded. "P-payment?"

"Stephanie will take your information, but Guardian will cover all the charges."

Sage stood and extended his left hand. They exchanged an awkward but sincere handshake, and

Sage started to leave. "Sage?" The man turned at the door.

"I know someone who may be able to help you with that stutter. My colleague, Doctor Wheeler."

The man smiled. "S-seeing him n-next M-Monday."

"Good. Stephanie's door is the last on the right and watch out for hidden branches."

Sage's laughter rumbled down the hall as he walked away. Zeke drew a breath and listened to Stephanie as she spoke with Sage. He could get used to hearing her voice, the quiet laughter, and the sound of her asking questions. The proximity made him happy. There was no other way to put it.

STEPHANIE WENT into the exam room. "Rusty, I can get your information now."

"Yes, ma'am." Rusty nodded and slipped off the exam table.

"Steph, I'm so sorry about the reception. Getting you to get all those supplies and then not using them." Gen said as she followed Rusty to Steph's office. Andrew was bringing up the rear. All four of them in the small office seemed almost claustrophobic. Steph sat down and frowned. "I used them. The weather caused the delay. I think the food will be fine. God knows it'll be cold enough in that basement."

"Wait, you decorated?" Gen popped off the wall where she'd been leaning.

"Yes! It looks nice if I do say so myself."

"I can't wait to see it." Gen spun. "Drew, do you think you can arrange it with Declan? We can still have the reception." Stephanie smiled as she watched Andrew melt under his bride's request. "I'll call him."

Gen squealed at his answer and popped on her toes to kiss him. Rusty shook his head. "These two have been at it since they got back from Denver. Hell, since they met, really."

Drew pulled out his phone and called Declan. He waited for a moment before he left a voice message. "Declan, this is Andrew. I'd like to talk to you about moving the reception date to the first day most of us are dug out. Give me a call." He glanced over at Stephanie. "Is it strange that it went to voicemail?"

"Not really. If I know my brother, he's outside shoveling his way to the snowblower." She'd call him later that afternoon and check on him. Stephanie woke up her computer and clicked on the form she needed to fill out. Getting Rusty's information was interesting. He knew the company Senior had insurance through, but not his policy number. Nor did he have his social security card with him or memorized. "When you return to the ranch, I'll need both to finish the paperwork."

She took the information and visited with them as they re-wrapped Rusty's hand for travel and bundled up to make the trip back to the Hollister ranch. Rusty's hand looked like a club, but Steph noticed the gentle way Gen took care of the hired hand. She was a good woman and a perfect match for Andrew.

Sage walked down the hall as Steph entered her office, and she took his information and filled out the form. He wrote down the things she needed, which sped the process along. After thanking her, he walked out of the clinic. Stephanie saved the document and turned off her computer. There wasn't much she could do without an internet connection.

She wandered down the hall and heard Zeke speaking. She stopped in the doorway and listened as he rambled off a slew of medical terminology. He stopped talking and clicked the mouse beside his keyboard. "Done with dictating my notes. Are you ready to go back to the house?" He smiled at her and leaned back in his chair.

"Sure, or I could work on that filing disaster you have over there." She nodded her head toward the cabinets that lined his office. She couldn't wait to get things in order and prove she could do the job.

"There will be plenty of time for that when the office opens. I'd rather play for the rest of the snow day." Zeke pulled her toward him and onto his lap.

"Is play a code word for sex?" She wrapped her arms around his neck, twisting her torso to face him.

Zeke blinked and wagged his head side to side. "It could be."

"We can come up with something more original." She squinted in concentration.

"Orange."

She groaned. "No. Just no. I hate that color."

"I know, I know, if you ever wear it, someone has forced you." Zeke laughed. "What about pumpkin? That could fit into daily conversation." He leaned and kissed her.

She dropped her arms and placed her hands on his chest, staring. "As long as you never, ever, call *me* that. I was traumatized." She leaned against his chest, and he wrapped her in his arms.

"Promise." He kissed the top of her head.

"Zeke?"

"Yeah?" He dropped his chin on top of her head.

"Is this real?" If it was a dream, she never wanted to wake up.

"It is. It's good, too." He squeezed her tighter for a moment.

"It is. I'm afraid it won't last," she admitted.

"I get that. We've both been burned in the past. You far worse than me, but I get where you're coming from. How about we just take this a day at a time and be happy now." He rubbed her back with one of his big hands.

She sighed and nodded against his chest. "I am. Happy." And that scared her more than anything else. She hadn't been happy in so long. The feeling was utterly foreign.

"I am, too. Let's get your shoes, bundle up, and go make some pumpkin pie."

Stephanie burst out laughing. "Lord, you'll need to work on using that code word."

16

"Hello." Declan sounded exasperated.

"Hey, you. How're things?" Stephanie sat on a chair in Zeke's weight room, watching as he lifted the heavyweights. Stripped down to a pair of shorts and a tank top, she could see his muscles flex and move under the strain of the exercise. Rather than jump him and make pumpkin pie again, she asked if she could call Declan with Zeke's cell. He'd recharged it with a portable battery pack he kept charged. The doctor was definitely organized in all areas except his filing systems.

"I fucking got high-centered trying to get to the road," Declan groaned.

"Why did you try to get to the road that night?

You could have gotten stuck somewhere between home and Hollister. And don't hurry getting it out of the snow bank. It's way too early for the road to be cleared." Zeke glanced at her with a concerned look on his face. She smiled and shook her head, letting him know everything was okay.

"I need to check on the Spur. Last year, I had to repair the roof, and I know I should have just gone with a whole new roof instead of just a repair." Declan was worked up. That bar was his baby.

"Declan, it was fine when I left. I'm sure it's okay. Phil is clearing the streets in the town. I can ask Zeke to take me over tomorrow morning and check to make sure it's okay."

"Yeah? Thanks. That's yeah. Thanks. She's my livelihood, you know?"

"She's your one true love." Stephanie poked at him.

"Maybe you're right. No one else seems to stick." Declan laughed.

"Only because you don't let them." She'd witnessed his morning brush-off too many times to count while living with him. "I'll call." Those words were the end of every one of his relationships.

He snorted. "Maybe. You doing all right?"

"We made fireplace stew and hardtack." She

glanced at Zeke. "And we've gotten to know each other better." A lot better. "Your friend is horrible at dominos."

Declan belted out a hardy laugh. "Don't tell me you took his money."

She scoffed. "No, we didn't bet."

"I'll come to get you as soon as the roads are clear," Declan said, suddenly serious. "I know you probably had concerns about staying with Zeke, but he's a decent man, Steph. You can trust him."

She smiled and looked over at Zeke, who was doing pull-ups. "He's a wonderful man, Dec."

"Uh-oh ... Did I hear what I think I just heard?"

"Maybe." She felt her face heat. "Probably."

"Is it mutual?" Declan's question was low as if they were sitting together at the kitchen table and talking in hushed tones.

"Yes. Very much so." She dropped her eyes. "He's ..." She looked at Zeke as he dropped to the floor and turned his gaze to her. "He's special. He makes me feel beautiful and happy."

Declan sighed. "You deserve both. Call me when you want me to come to get you."

"I have dad's truck. I'll get it jumped if I need to, but I'll bring it home. Shouldn't be more than a day or so."

"That sounds about right. Andrew Hollister called twice after leaving a voicemail. He's offered to pay my nightly intake for the nights I can't open because of your decorations, so they can have a reception."

"Wow, that's kind of excessive." She blinked at the thought of how much that would cost Andrew.

"I said no. I told him to consider it a wedding gift." Declan cleared his throat. "He used to be a damn good friend."

"He still could be if you dropped your anger." She watched Zeke lay on the weight bench under a bar loaded with weights.

"Well, damn it, I had to be mad at someone, and it wasn't going to be you." The gruff words were sweet in the typical Declan way.

"I love you, too. Be safe and be careful when you try to dig out the truck."

"How did you know I was going to dig out the truck?"

"Because I was raised with you. I'll check the Spur tomorrow and give you a call."

"Text me, okay? My battery is low, and I'm not sure it will make it until morning. I'll charge it in the truck tomorrow when I'm shoveling."

"That works. But you text or call if you need help, okay?"

"I will. I'm not stupid. Lived here all my life. I know how to work in this weather. Hey, by the way, I'm happy for you and Zeke."

"Thank you."

"Night, brat." Declan hung up before she could say another word.

"He okay?" Zeke grunted the question as he pushed up the weights.

"Fine. He high-centered his truck and is going to dig it out tomorrow. He's freaking about the Spur. If the roads are clear, could you drive me over tomorrow, so I can tell him it didn't collapse in the snowstorm?"

Zeke put the bar back in the rest over his head. His arms dropped down. "Sure. You said the bar was his one true love. Really?"

"So far, yep." She laughed. "Some day, one of those women he brings home will grab ahold and not let go. Until then, his bar is his life. He'd probably build a house behind it if he didn't have the land that Mom and Dad left us."

Zeke started to say something when the lights flickered and then stayed on. "Electricity," he said instead. "Time to go to work." He wiped his sweaty brow. “I need to inspect the water lines and figure out where it froze this time.”

“What can I do to help?” She stood up, ready to do whatever he needed her to do.

“Put the fridge back in order? I’ll crank the heat and warm up the house.” He stood up, and she let her eyes linger. “I’d be freezing in a pair of shorts.”

He chuckled. “I worked up a sweat.”

“The visual is not lost on me.” She smiled at him.

“Good to know.” He walked over and lifted her off the chair. She wrapped her legs around his waist and her arms around his neck. “But we need to do a few things before we make more pumpkin pie.”

She tossed back her head and laughed. “Seriously, we need a different term.”

ZEKE WOKE in his own bed with a cloud of blonde curls spread across his chest. He blinked the sleep out of his eyes and tried to figure out what position Stephanie had contorted herself into. Her feet were off the side of the bed, and her head was wedged between his arm and ribs. He lifted his head and glanced down at her. Her long blonde lashes rested on her freckleless cheeks. Her lips were slightly parted as she slept. Seeing her so relaxed fed his inner caveman. He wanted to protect her from the assholes of the world. He dropped his head and played with a lock of her hair, running his fingers through it. The attraction he'd felt for her had grown into serious feelings. It was too soon. He knew he'd scare her away if he made any stupid declarations. But one day, he'd place a ring on her finger. She'd be worth any wait. Hell, his mom hadn't found Pete until she was almost fifty.

"G'morning," Steph mumbled and stretched, burrowing deeper into his side.

He turned and waited for her to open her eyes. She blinked them open, tipped her head backward, and smiled at him. "Hi."

"Hey. Your feet are off the bed."

She lifted her head and looked at her feet. "Why?"

"Because you move around when you sleep." He'd stirred throughout the night when she tossed and turned. Not because she was moving, but because he wasn't used to anyone in his bed, and the movement woke him.

"Did I keep you awake? I'm sorry. I didn't mean to do that."

He lifted onto his elbow so she could see him

without tipping her head back. “No. You didn’t do anything wrong. You don’t have to apologize.”

She closed her eyes. “I’m afraid that’s my default.”

“We’ll work on changing that.” He bent down and kissed her.

“We should make some pie.” She teased him when he lifted.

“I’d love to, but unfortunately, snow days are over, and it’s almost eight-thirty. We need to be to work by nine.”

Stephanie’s naked form popped off the bed. “Oh, crud! I don’t have any work clothes here. I need to go home.”

“Steph.” Zeke tried to interrupt.

“I don’t think I can make it in thirty minutes.” She picked up his shirt and tossed it to the chair beside the bed. “Where’s my bra?”

“Stephanie,” Zeke said a bit louder.

She froze and looked over at him, her eyes wide and terrified. “Hey, no, I was just trying to get your attention. I put your clothes in the washer last night after you fell asleep. Just pop them in the dryer. They’ll be dry in time.”

“You did that? For me?”

Zeke frowned. "Well, yeah. You were exhausted. Why wouldn't I?"

Steph pushed her hair out of her face. "It's just that ... I haven't had many people look out for me."

Zeke nodded. "I get that. You get in the shower, and I'll put your clothes in the dryer."

A smile spread across her face. "Thank you."

"You're welcome. Now, hustle, woman, or we'll both be late." Zeke smiled when she moved around the bed and bent down to kiss him. "We'll make pie tonight."

He nodded. "I'll come to your place, and we'll make sure it made it through the storm."

"Good idea." She kissed him. "Safety first."

He kissed her, tasting her unique flavor he swore he'd never get enough of. He pulled her into bed with him, and she laughed, "What about work and my clothes?"

He groaned and flopped onto his back. She rested on his chest. "Pumpkin pie tonight."

"But I'm starving now." And yeah, that sounded whiny as hell.

"How can you be? We had a lot of pie last night."

"I'll never have enough."

She smiled at him. "I have the same hunger."

Zeke growled and started to wrap his arms around her. “No. Work, then pie.” She slipped out of his arms and padded across the carpeted floor into the bathroom. Zeke groaned and draped his arm over his eyes. “Clothes!” Stephanie called from the bathroom.

“Right.” He threw the blankets off and looked down at his semi-hard and downright pissed-off cock. “Later, dude. Later.” He slid out of bed and headed to the laundry room. Who could imagine that dessert had become his favorite meal of the day?

17

Zeke finished his notes on the patient he'd just seen and stared out the window at the white-coated scenery. He spun at a knock at his door. "Well, got yourself dug out, did you?"

Jeremiah Wheeler nodded. "It took a full day and a half. That storm dumped on us, didn't it?"

"It did a bang-up job. I met a soon-to-be patient of yours yesterday." Zeke nodded to one of the chairs in his office. They weren't the big comfy chairs Jeremiah had in his office for his patients, but they worked for Zeke.

Jeremiah's brow furrowed. "Who would that be?"

"Sage Browning. He fell, and a branch decided to embed itself in his hand."

"Is the injury serious?" Jeremiah's tone changed immediately.

"Not unless it gets infected. Worried?"

Jeremiah got up and closed the door. "I noticed Stephanie was working, and this isn't for public dissemination. It took almost two years to get Sage back into the fold. He suffers from a TBI, which caused the stuttering, but he's been through the wringer. I haven't had my assessment with him yet and need to find a ground zero, so we can work on his issues."

Zeke shrugged. "Other than his stuttering, I didn't notice any issues. He has a snarky sense of humor and seems empathetic. He went out in the snow looking for a teenager who got turned around and found him."

Jeremiah nodded. "Which fits with his profile. Thanks for the information. What's the town scuttle-butt? Eden wanted to come in, but I wasn't sure if the highways would be clear."

"Are they?" Zeke asked.

"For the most part, yep. I noticed a few trucks parked in turnouts, so people are digging out. It's clear from my place to here."

"So Steph can make it home tonight." Zeke nodded.

"Yes ... Where has she been?" Jeremiah cocked his head.

Zeke looked him in the eye. "With me."

"With you ... or *with* you?" A bit of a smile ticked up the corner of Jeremiah's lips.

"We're together." Zeke acknowledged the fact. "She doesn't work for us. She works for Dori down in Belle. Not a conflict of interest."

"Dude, did I say a thing?" Jeremiah held up his hands in surrender.

"Sorry." He rubbed his face. "We got serious fast, but damn it, I've been attracted since I first saw her."

"Well, she's strikingly beautiful." Jeremiah agreed.

Zeke looked up at him. "Yeah, but when she's not wearing all that makeup and lets her hair curl, she's gorgeous. But more than that, she's good here." He placed his hand on his heart.

"Has the mighty Zeke Johnson finally found *the one*?" Jeremiah teased.

"I should flip you off for that comment, but in truth, I think I have." Zeke leaned back in his chair. "Now the goal is not to fuck up the relationship until she believes the same thing."

"Difference of opinion already?" Jeremiah cocked his head.

"No, I'm just not pushing her." He glanced at the door. "She was the victim of domestic violence, and I'm not going to pressure her."

Jeremiah blinked at him and shifted in his chair. "I could talk with her."

"No. I told you this so you wouldn't make a joke or a random comment. If she wants to talk with you in a professional capacity, she'll approach you. Give her time. Plus, you need to have some background about the woman working in the front office. This is privileged information between us."

"Of course, as always," Jeremiah replied immediately.

The phone on Zeke's desk rang, and he reached for it. "Doctor Johnson."

"Hey, Zeke, it's Adam. Just wanted to let you know we're home. We landed in Rapid this morning, and I'm here at the ranch."

"The highways are open?"

"To the Rocking M, at least. It was slow going, but a couple of SUVs were on the road along with us. Anything of note happen while I was gone?"

"It snowed like crazy," Zeke deadpanned. "Other than that, nothing of note except I treated one of yours." He told Adam the specifics of Sage's injuries and how he got them.

"Good to know. I haven't met him yet, but I hear he's a good guy."

"Seemed to be. You need anything out there?"

"Nope, we're set. I'll give you a call as soon as we dig out, and we can work a rotation, so I don't have to drag this phone around twenty-four seven. Until then, if you need anything, you give me a call."

"I think we have it covered, but I will keep you in mind." Zeke ended the call and glanced over at Jeremiah. "I think he's bored."

"Probably, but that'll end soon enough. That organization can move mountains, and when they do, people get injured. Just a fact."

"That's the truth. I'm happy to fill in for him. Lord knows things around here are hit and miss."

"Careful, Guardian has a way of sucking you in and making you one of them." Jeremiah chuckled and stood up. "I'm going to head over to the store, and if Ciera can get into the diner, pick up some food that Eden doesn't have to cook. She's got the flu."

Zeke winced. "Which means the kids and you will be next. Need anything?"

"Nope. Going to get some over-the-counter meds and the meals from the diner, so the kids and I don't have to survive on my cooking. If I call out, you'll know why."

"Food poisoning. Got it." Zeke laughed when Jeremiah flipped him off. "Seriously, no problem. Steph will call and reschedule your people if you need her to."

Jeremiah shook his head. "I haven't let my patients know there'll be someone working with me. Some are pretty skittish, so I'll make the calls until I can let them know. You know how it is."

"I do." A few of Jeremiah's clients balanced on a tightrope on good days. On bad, they hung on for dear life. Messing with their normal wasn't a good thing.

"Tell Steph to get out to their place before it gets too dark. The black ice is horrible, and no one will see her vehicle until morning if she goes into a ditch. She hasn't been around for one of these storms in years."

"Damn good point. Tell Eden I hope she feels better."

"Will do." Jeremiah left, and Zeke looked at the clock. It was almost three. There wouldn't be much more daylight.

He made his way to the front to find Stephanie on

the phone. "So, the second screen isn't needed unless we need to file a primary and a secondary insurance, such as Medicaid Part B or a supplemental rider?" She smiled up at him as he entered. "Perfect, thanks, Dori. No, no worries at all. Driving up here isn't safe. Uh-huh. I'll call if I have any questions. Thanks again." She hung up the phone. "The software isn't that different from the one I used before. There were a couple of screens I didn't understand, so I called her. I've got all of today's patients pushed through, and I'll complete yesterday's paperwork now."

Zeke leaned down and kissed her. "You're going to whip us into shape in no time."

"Better watch out. We'll be highly efficient." Steph laughed.

"But not today." Zeke sat on her desk.

"Why?"

"Jeremiah said the black ice was wicked on the highway. You might want to get out of here and home before dark. You don't have chains on your dad's truck. Has Declan called to let you know the road to your place was open?"

"No, but when I called him to tell him his beloved Spur was in one piece, he was almost done digging out his truck. He was going to clear a path to my house, so I could get to it easier. If he isn't at the bar, he's sound asleep after digging out."

"I'll drive you to the Spur and return for my four o'clock."

"Oh, here's the clipboard with the intake forms. I've highlighted the areas they need to fill out, and I have cards printed with our office number so they can call back with any information they don't have. That way, you can give them this and not have to bring them back to your office. I'll deal with the follow-up in the morning."

Zeke looked from the form to the card and the clipboard with a pen taped to a chain and attached to the board. "Wow."

"You're paying me to make this easier for you, right?" The smile that lit up her face was a beautiful thing to behold. He put the clipboard on the desk and lifted her from her chair. She squealed and laughed. He spun her around just because he loved hearing her laughter. She grabbed his shoulders and dropped a kiss on his lips. When they parted, she stared at him. "You'll call Declan's cell before you come out? Just in case that black ice strikes?"

"I will." He dropped her and bent for one final kiss. "Let's get you to your truck and on the way, so I can get back in case Mrs. Dunbar is early. Hey, I'm serious. You've done a wonderful job here today." He'd resolved to build her up with the truth. To acknowledge the good in her, the hard work, and the things she could be proud of.

She smiled up at him. "Yeah?"

"Yeah. I really appreciate and am pleased with what you've done so far."

She blinked, and her eyes misted up. "Thank you. No one has said that in a long time."

He bent down to kiss her again. "I'll always tell you."

"Always is a long time." She stared up at him.

Zeke smiled at her. "Not when you're with the right person."

18

Watching Zeke in her rearview mirror, Stephanie smiled as he lifted a hand again. Her dad's old truck had to be jumped, and then they shoveled a bit to get it out of its parking spot. It was getting dark, and low clouds obscured the setting sun, but Stephanie didn't care. The thrill of being important to Zeke carried her through the drive home. She drove slowly. There was no one on the road, which was usual. Slowing to turn into the drive that would lead to her place and Declan's, she stopped. Declan's truck was still on the side of the road, although it looked like he'd freed it from the snowbank. She stopped and got out. The door was open, and Declan's phone was in the cab, attached to the charger. She saw several missed calls.

"What are you doing, Dec?" Steph pocketed the phone and got back into her father's truck. She trundled down the snow-packed drive. There was a set of tracks leading into the property. She saw why when she turned the corner and cleared the tree claim. A black SUV was parked in front of Declan's house. When her headlights illuminated the area next to the old place, she could tell that Declan hadn't cleared a path to her house.

A sense of frustration nipped at her. "Great." She put the truck into park and turned off the engine. Staring at his house, she muttered, "Declan, if you are playing sex God right now ..." She got out, shut the door, and fought through the snow to the small cleared area in front of his house. "I'll call Zeke and spend the night there," she grumbled and stamped off her shoes before she opened the door.

"Declan—" The door was jerked out of her hand as someone grabbed a handful of her hair. She lost her balance and was slammed to the floor, the hand in her hair propelling her down. Turning quickly to avert, she slammed her chin into the hardwood. Her cheek took all the impact, making her face explode in pain. She gasped and froze when she heard the voice.

"You fucking country bumpkin bitch. You stole

from me! After everything I gave you?" Her head was lifted again and then driven to the floor. She felt the warmth of blood, although the pain was so intense she couldn't tell where it was coming from.

"I didn't take anything!"

Presley's knee landed on her back between her shoulders. He put all of his weight on her. "Where's my fucking car, cunt?" He pulled her up, and she gasped, but not from the pain that time. "Answer me, or Roland will gut your fucking brother."

Declan, God, Declan! Her brother was tied to a kitchen chair, and someone had beaten him. There was dried blood under his nose and around his mouth. His face was so bruised his eyes were almost swollen shut. "No. Let him go."

"Show her."

Stephanie screamed as Roland sliced Declan's face splitting his cheek open. "Stop! I'll take you to it."

"Steph, no!" Declan shook his head, blood from his fresh wound staining his flannel shirt.

Presley jerked her up. "Talk now, and maybe I won't make your brother watch while I teach you a lesson, my little whore." Pressley shook her, then lifted her to her feet by her hair. She didn't try to fight him. God knew it would only make him more volatile. He pressed his face next to her ear and spoke through clenched teeth. "You know what was in that car? Eighty kilos of uncut Fentanyl, you stupid bitch. Street market on that load will make me a fucking billionaire."

"There was nothing in the car! I promise, there was nothing." She closed her eyes when she saw the movement. His backhand sent her flying against the wall. Explosions of red and black mushroomed behind her eyes, and she slid to the floor. Presley started pacing until his black slacks and shoes stopped in front of her.

He squatted in front of her and raged, "You stupid cunt! It's in the frame of the car. You better know where that fucking car is."

"Steph—" Declan began, but Stephanie interrupted him.

"In Belle Fourche. I put it in a storage unit. I didn't want anyone to see it in case you reported it as stolen."

She couldn't let Presley get his hands on the drugs. If he did, both she and Declan would be dead. If she lured him and his men away from Hollister, maybe Declan could get some help. It was their only chance. She glanced around the room. Roland, Harris, and Claude. His most trusted.

"Steph, no." Declan stared at her through the slits in his eyelids.

"I'll take you. But you have to leave him. Alive." She forced herself up. Presley could kill her, but she was damned if she let the bastard kill Declan.

"You have no room to bargain, bitch. You told me all I need to know."

"No, I didn't. I know you, Presley. I knew you'd kill him and then me if I told you. It isn't in Belle, but it is south of here. South of there. Kill me, and you'll never find it. Kill him, and I'll never tell you."

The backhand was so quick she didn't even see it coming. Her head exploded in pain from Presley's punch before the other side connected to the wall. The next thing she knew, Claude was shaking her awake.

"Tie him. I don't care if his fucking hands and feet fall off. He doesn't have a chance of moving. Understand?" Presley shouted at Roland and Harris.

"Get that bitch into the car." Claude started to drag her to her feet when Declan's cell phone rang. Claude snatched it out of her coat and tossed it to Presley.

"Doctor Johnson?" Presley looked between her and Declan.

"He's the local doctor. Everyone was worried

about Declan because he didn't answer his cell phone. I took it out of the truck when I came in just now. If I don't answer, he'll show up with our neighbors. People take care of each other out here. Please let me call him. I don't want anyone else hurt."

Presley tossed the phone to Claude. "Put it on speaker. I want to hear every word." He moved over to Declan and took the butcher knife they'd used earlier to slice her brother's cheek. "One wrong word, and he dies." Presley pushed the knife against Declan's neck.

Claude hit redial, and Stephanie spoke as soon as she heard the line connect. She knew her voice was shaking and hoped that Zeke would understand her. "Doctor Johnson, this is Stephanie. I found Declan. Don't worry. He's okay. He's been busy moving snow."

Zeke didn't say anything for a minute. "Are you okay?"

"Yeah, I am, just shivering from the cold. Don't worry about us. I'm going to drive down to Belle tonight and spend the night at the Dakota Lodge. I want to be there in the morning to buy that orange coat I kept telling Donna Franks about. I love it so much. So you won't see us for the next couple of days."

Zeke's voice took on an odd tone. *He knew. He knew she was in trouble.* "I remember you saying how much you like the color orange. Is Declan going with you?"

Presley's narrowed gaze cut through her like lasers as he listened for anything that sounded like her asking for help. "No, he's going to see his girlfriend. I better go."

"So, he's not coming to the Spur tonight?"

"No, you know him. He hates that place. He's tied up with all the snow and then driving over to the Marshall ranch to see Keelee. Tell Ken he'll have to have a drink without him tonight."

"All right. I'll do that. Take care of yourself."

"Yeah. Bye." Stephanie waited for Claude to kill the connection and didn't dare look at Declan. He had to have registered the insanity of the call.

"Get that fucking bitch in the SUV. Make sure he's not going anywhere."

Presley stopped at the thermostat on the wall. He flicked the switch off and glanced back at Declan. "Freeze to death, you motherfucker."

19

Zeke dropped his phone on the bench of his truck. What the fuck. He drew a deep breath and thought through the conversation again. She was in trouble. She was going south, to Belle and Declan ... and Keelee? What the ... Fuck, she was asking for Guardian's help.

Zeke fumbled with his phone when he picked it up to call Adam. "Need me already?" Adam laughed into the connection.

"Adam, I have a situation here."

All the laughter was gone in an instant. "What do you need?"

"That's it. I don't know. I just had the strangest conversation with Stephanie. She went home tonight. But something's wrong."

"Calm down. Tell me the conversation, word for word."

"She talked before I could say a word, you know, kind of in a panic. She said she found Declan and that he was okay."

"That's not distressing," Adam interjected.

"No, in itself, it isn't. I got a feeling in my gut. I asked if she was okay. She said she was, and she was shivering from the cold, but then she said that she was going to drive down to Belle tonight, that she wanted to be there to purchase an orange coat that she told Donna Franks about and that I probably wouldn't see her for the next couple days."

"I don't see the problem?" Adam led him.

"She despises the color orange and would never wear it. Ever. Donna Franks was the gossip that drove her out of town. Plus, she lives with her daughter, not here in Hollister."

Adam finally agreed, "Yes, that's weird. I have to ask you something, Zeke. Does Stephanie drink or do drugs?"

"What? Hell no!" Zeke raged.

"Chill, brother, I had to ask, you know what I'm talking about. What else did she say?"

"I asked if Declan was going with her, and she said no, he was going to see his girlfriend, Keelee at the Marshall Ranch. I asked if he was going to the Spur, and she said no, he hated the place and that I should tell Ken to have a drink without him."

"Fuck. She's in trouble," Adam agreed. "What do you know about her? Her background? Who would want to hurt her or Declan?"

"Fuck. She just got out of a physically abusive relationship with some guy in Denver. Presley something."

"I'm going to need more than that, my friend," Adam said. "Do you think there were any police reports about the abuse?"

"No, she was too afraid. Wait. Declan was doing some digging on the guy. She found a file at his office at the Spur."

"Get over there and get me that name. I'm running this information to Mike."

"Mike? Why?" He knew the guy. He did something at the complex.

"He runs this place," Adam said quickly. "Call me. I'll get to work on this end."

"I need to go out there. Maybe there's something I can do."

Adam snapped, "Dude, you can go out there and get yourself into a hell of a mess and be part of the problem, or you can listen to me and help Stephanie and Declan. Your choice."

"Fuck!" Zeke yelled and slammed his hand against the steering wheel.

"Zeke, is Stephanie more than an acquaintance?" Adam's voice cut through his rage at being unable to help.

He shoved the gear selector into first and popped the clutch on his truck. He growled out the words, "She's mine."

"Go get that information. We'll meet you at the Spur in ten minutes." He could hear Adam running.

Zeke shifted through his gears. "There's no way you can be here in ten minutes."

"Just wait for us there." The barked order was one he sure as fuck didn't want to follow.

Zeke didn't bother to hang up, instead shoving the phone into his pocket. His truck skated through the parking lot of the Spur when he hit the brakes. Before it came to a complete stop, he threw the truck into neutral and stomped on the emergency brake. Leaving the door open and the truck running, he bolted from the cab.

The front doors were blocked by snow and dead-bolted, so he bypassed them and made his way to the back of the bar. There were two high windows—

the bathrooms. He passed them. A window, with chicken wire reinforcing the glass, was next. That was either a store room or Declan's office. Zeke ran back to his truck, grabbed a crowbar, and sprinted back to the rear of the joint. He shoved the claw end of the bar into the base of the window and pushed down with all his weight.

The window groaned, then shattered. He moved the bar and pried again, and the wood at the bottom broke. Zeke used the crowbar and slashed down on the chicken wire, bending it in. The second slam broke it, and he grabbed one side with the claw, ripping it back and out. He did the same with the other side and pushed, then cleared the remaining jagged edges of the glass. He threw the crowbar into the room and hefted himself through the window.

He landed on a case of Scotch and rolled onto his feet. Storeroom. He made his way to the door. The fucker was locked ... from the outside. Zeke reared back and focused all his rage and worry on the door handle. The kick broke the door, and the top half splintered, hanging from the hinges. Zeke kicked the bottom of the door twice to clear it before he entered the hall. He'd never been to the back part of the bar and had no idea where Declan's office was. Choosing to go to the right, he jogged down the hall.

He opened the doors. Janitor's closet, storage, storage. *What the fuck was with all the storage in this place?*

The last door opened, and he flipped on the light switch. Bingo. He sprinted to the desk and grabbed files. Invoice, bills, bank statements. Zeke slapped a brown folder down and opened it.

He pulled his phone from his pocket and hit redial. "What do you have?"

"Presley Cheston. Denver, Colorado. Cheston Enterprises. There are photos here. He's always with the three same guys. They look like a protection detail."

"That's enough. We're almost there now."

"What?" Zeke asked the question, but the line was dead. He picked up an enlarged grainy picture of the bastard that had beat Stephanie. God help him, but his oath to do no harm would not stop him from giving that man a taste of what he'd put Stephanie through.

Zeke stopped and listened. *What the ... A helicopter?* He grabbed the folder and sprinted to the front of the bar. He threw the deadbolt and opened the door, shoving his way through the three-foot snow drift blown against the door during the storm. He walked out into the open and looked up. A flashing light to his southwest grew brighter.

A fucking helicopter. He blinked and strained when he saw two sets of lights. Two? He shoved the folder into his coat and, as the helicopters drew closer, moved to the side of the building to protect himself from the sting of the blowing ice and snow when the copters landed.

Adam and Mike sprinted from one copter. Mike yelled to him. "One team is going to get Declan. The other is going south, assuming that this bastard is taking your woman as she said."

"I'm going south." Hopefully, Declan would be all right, but his gut told him Stephanie was the one in trouble.

"Go with Adam." Mike ran to the other chopper. Zeke ducked and ran to the other aircraft, following Adam.

"Here." He didn't hear the words but saw Adam say them as he handed Zeke a headset. "Can you hear me?"

"Yes." Zeke acknowledged. "I brought this."

He handed the folder to Adam. The man looked at the documents. Zeke glanced up and saw two men he didn't recognize. They both carried rifles that looked like they were made for a jungle expedition. Both of them nodded, and he nodded back. Fuck, he was glad he called Adam. "Alpha Five to Alpha Two."

Zeke did a double take at Adam. He recognized Chief's voice answering Adam's call. "This is Alpha Two. Go."

"Looks like this asshole travels with security. Be careful on your approach."

"Roger," Chief responded.

"Alpha Five, this is CCS," a woman's voice came across the headset,

"Go," Adam said.

The woman continued. "I ran the name Presley Cheston. His photo hit on the DEA and ICE databases. He's wanted for the murder of three men during a border skirmish twelve years ago. They have him on video. Execution-style murder. His real name is Paul Little. He has a list of warrants. No contact with law enforcement since the border incident. Alpha One and Archangel relate you have permission to take this jerk into custody. The FBI, ICE, DEA, and the state police have been advised that this is a Guardian operation. The FBI will take control when they arrive on scene."

"ETA on FBI?" Adam snapped the question.

"Tomorrow evening. Your op, Alpha Five." The woman relayed the information, and Zeke could swear he heard typing in the background as she spoke.

"Have the state police block all traffic northbound on Highway 85."

"Copy that," the woman said, and the headphones went silent for a moment.

"Drake, swing out wide. I want to see where they are. Then we'll find a nice hill."

"Damn straight. Just like Afghanistan." The pilot lifted a gloved hand and gave a thumbs up.

"Exactly," Adam confirmed.

One of the large men across from him spoke. "Are we to take out the vehicle or the driver?"

"Disable the vehicle. We have a Guardian onboard."

Zeke looked over at Adam. The man shrugged. "We pay her salary. She's one of us. Just like you."

"Alpha Two, Alpha Five."

"Go."

"We have Declan. He needs medical but is ambulatory."

"Take him to the Annex. We'll be there as soon as possible."

"Copy. Whatever it takes."

"As long as it takes." Every person on the helicopter except Zeke spoke the words.

Zeke looked over at the man who appeared to be more than just a doctor. "I wasn't in Afghanistan. What's going to happen?"

Adam smiled at him. "A big surprise. When we determine where they are ..."

20

Stephanie inched away from Preston. She prayed Zeke understood her. Declan needed help. God only knew what they'd done to him. She moved a bit farther, and Presley grabbed her hair, pulling her back against him. "Move again, and I'll take out some of my anger on you." He kept his hand in her hair, pulling it so hard she cried. "Imagine my surprise when I returned, and you were gone. I didn't really care. You're too much damn work, but my car? I'll make you regret stealing from me."

"I didn't know there were drugs in the car."

"You stupid bitch, no one knows drugs are in that car. That's why I use it." He pushed her down, her nose against his knee. "I killed James. He swore he brought the car back. Swore it until his dying breath. When Claude found you gone, I assumed you just ran away. Why would I think you'd take my mule?"

"I didn't know!" She felt the soft tissue in her nose crack when her head struck his knee. The bone broke when he lifted his knee and shoved her head down again.

"You lived in that house for years. You knew. How could you not? You're ignorant, not stupid. Did you hide it until you could figure out what to do with the drugs?"

"I don't want anything to do with drugs." When she spoke, the blood from her nose seeped into her mouth. The copper taste wasn't new.

"But you want the money," Presley growled, shoving her nose harder onto his knee.

"No," she cried but didn't beg him to stop. It would only make him hurt her more.

"How far is it to that fucking town?" Presley spat the question.

"About another hour, boss," Roland answered.

"You picked a good place to hide. I would have never found you if your brother hadn't hired that moron of a private investigator. He was digging too deep. I eliminated him, but not before discovering why he was trailing me and who paid for it. Imagine my surprise when your brother's name popped up in that conversation. It was just a matter of a quick search after that. If the fucking snowstorm hadn't hit, I'd have been here days ago." Presley's hand relaxed in her hair, but she didn't move, didn't try to ease the pain. It was one of the times she tried to disappear in plain sight. Preston shouted, "Can you fucking drive faster?"

"There's ice, boss. We hit a patch going too fast, and we'll be in the ditch," Roland said from the driver's seat.

"I said to go faster." Presley's hand gripped her hair tightly again.

Stephanie felt the vehicle accelerate as Presley pushed her away. "Bitch, you bled on my slacks." He kicked her on her calf. She huddled away from him and curled into a ball on the seat.

"Why isn't there any traffic?" Presley mused.

"Pretty remote place and the storm," Claude answered.

"Who would want to be out here," Harris added. "This is a shithole."

Presley chuckled. "A shithole for my piece of shit woman. Fitting. Sit up, you whore." Presley hit her on the back with a closed fist punch. She did as he asked. Her face and neck were sticky with blood, and her back and lower leg ached. She stifled a groan. Steph sat up in the seat and looked out the window. The rolling hills had become more prominent and would only get bigger the farther south they drove.

What are you going to tell him when we get to Belle? Where can I say the car is? Someplace populated? Maybe I'll be able to call out for help? Rapid City. But where? Maybe the mall parking lot? What time is it? Will the mall be closed when we get there? God, will I make it out of this alive? She stared forward as they crested a hill.

As brilliant light flooded the vehicle, Stephanie heard Roland and Claud shouting. Harris yelled from behind them. The vehicle jerked to the right, and Stephanie grabbed for her seatbelt. Presley screamed words she couldn't understand. Buckle. Buckle. The seatbelt snapped into place seconds before the tire hit the edge of the shoulder. Stephanie tucked her knees to her chest and placed her arms over her head. The sound of the vehicle hitting the snow echoed in her ears. The SUV rolled, cracking all the windows on the driver's side. The top caved in, and the passenger's side windows shattered before the SUV came to rest on its tires.

Stephanie felt Presley grab her hair, but she was buckled in. He screamed at her, hit her with something, and then the belt was free. "Get up there and kill whoever did this."

Stephanie fell into the snow at Presley's feet. Her ears filled with a roar, and she looked up to see the brilliant light edging over the bank. *A helicopter?* The wind from the propellors chucked ice crystals that had formed on the snow banks at them with enough force to cut through her skin. Presley and his guards started shooting. The light peeled away. "Kill them!" Presley shouted and grabbed her by the hair. "This way, bitch. Harris with me."

Presley half dragged, half pulled her up to the road while Roland and Claud started firing on the helicopter. Two loud reports stopped all the shooting, and Presley stopped. "Harris, you stop them from following me."

"Where are you going?" Stephanie asked as he yanked her along. "You'll freeze to death!"

"Shut up!" He yanked her hair so hard that she fell down.

"Presley, stop!"

"Stop? Stop? You dare tell me to stop?" He pushed her away from him and pointed the gun at her. "Where's my fucking mule? Tell me or die now."

Steph stared up at the man who had caused her so much pain. She shook her head. Out of the corner of her eye, she saw movement, and she turned to watch as Zeke flew through the air and tackled Presley. They went down the ditch, and Stephanie scrambled toward the edge of the road. "Hey, I got you."

She fought to be released. "Zeke! Zeke! He has a gun!"

"Honey, I don't think that matters too much now." The big man that picked her up in his arms glanced at her face and grimaced. "Aw, man, now I gotta have a turn at that fucker. Why do assholes beat on women?"

"What?" Steph looked up at him. "Who are you?"

The guy shrugged. "A friend." He carried her over to the edge of the road.

ZEKE TUCKED and rolled as he and that son of a bitch tumbled down the ditch. He was on his feet before the bastard. Zeke stepped forward and kicked the man as he tried to stand. Oh, yeah, it was the fucker in the photo. No doubt about it, it was Presley. It was the man who beat Stephanie. The man who'd executed three men and the man responsible for whatever injuries Declan had received.

Zeke saw the gun fly from the man's hand. *Good. A fair fight*. He waited for Presley to get to his feet. "Who the fuck are you?"

Zeke jabbed with his left, which Presley blocked, but the man didn't block his right uppercut. Presley's jaw snapped shut, and his head hit the snow. "Get up!" Zeke urged the man.

"Who the fuck are you?" The words were slow and slurred. Presley's lip was cut, and he was bleeding. *Not enough*.

"Come on. Is that all you got?" Zeke baited the man. "Weak when you're not hitting women?"

A sneer spread across Presley's face. "She likes it."

And that was all Zeke had to hear. He stepped in and laid two punches to the man's gut. Presley got a glancing blow to the side of Zeke's head, but Zeke ducked the follow-up and countered with a left jab to the face and a right uppercut as Presley began to fall. The man hit the snow again, but he didn't move that time. Zeke wiped his brow and watched to make sure the fucker was breathing. It was the doctor in him. He shouldn't care, but he did.

"Zeke!" He looked up when Stephanie shouted his name. One of the men from the helicopter held her in his arms.

"Are you all right?" Zeke called.

She said something.

"What?" He stumbled forward.

The man yelled down the embankment, "She is now." Stephanie lifted a hand, and it dropped down into her lap.

Zeke looked back at the man who'd caused the woman he loved so much pain. "If I weren't a doctor, you'd be dead. Come on, you son of a bitch." Zeke grabbed Presley's foot and started to drag him up the hill. "Andrew knew what the fuck he was doing." He mumbled to himself. "Only Andrew had a fucking horse." He looked back at Presley. "You're a heavy bastard. I'm buying a horse." He worked both of them back up the ditch they'd tumbled down.

"Is he dead?" Stephanie asked nobody in particular.

"Nah, but I have a feeling he's going to wish he was." The Guardian chuckled. Zeke pulled one last time and then dropped Presley's leg. He extended his arms, and the Guardian carefully settled Stephanie into them. Zeke stared at the bruising on her face and her nose. God, it had to be broken. "Oh, fuck, baby."

"I'm okay. He's done worse." She watched the

Guardian pick up Presley's leg and drag him back toward the helicopter. She jumped. "Declan?"

"We've got him. He's going to the clinic out at the Marshall Ranch, and so are you."

"I hate hospitals." She leaned against him. "You heard me. You knew Presley was there."

"I know you hate hospitals, babe, but I promise it is just a clinic. And I'll always hear you."

"Always. Please, God, let it be always." She dropped her head against his chest, and he kissed the top of her head and started toward the helicopter.

"Zeke, I need some help." The second Guardian stepped up to him. "I'll take her to the helicopter."

Zeke looked down at her. Her bruises couldn't hide the look in her eyes. "Go, help them," she told him. Zeke nodded and let the Guardian take Stephanie from his arms.

"What do we have?" he asked Adam, who was working on one of Presley's men nearby. The other lay next to them, unmoving.

"Three GSWs. That one is a through and through. Stable. This one is a compound fracture. I've applied a tourniquet. I think the bullet nicked the femoral artery. Can you find a clamp?"

Zeke dug through Adam's kit. "The other?" He

handed a clamp to Adam and watched as the man maneuvered inside the wound and applied the clamp.

Adam sat back. "Drake, we need to get to the clinic, stat."

Drake and the Guardian who'd taken Stephanie to the helicopter were there with a stretcher. The other Guardian was assisting the other wounded asshole to the helicopter. Thankfully, the bastard was zip tied.

"That one is DRT," Adam said as they stood up and grabbed equipment.

"DRT?"

"Dead right there," Adam explained.

Zeke moved at a rapid clip with Adam to the helicopter. "You know the term DOA still works."

Adam shoved his bag in, and they took up position on either side of Stephanie, with the injured, unconscious, and dead criminals sandwiched on the floor between them and the Guardians who'd accompanied them.

Adam put on his headgear and gave a set to Steph. Zeke put on the headset he'd worn earlier before he wrapped a possessive arm around his woman.

Adam's voice came across the headset. "Alpha

Five to CCS. We have primary secured and four targets. One DOA, three trauma, all in custody."

"Copy that Alpha Five," the woman's voice came over the connection again.

"Thank you." Zeke held out a hand to the man across from him. "I'm Zeke. This is Stephanie," he said, motioning toward her.

Her face was swollen, and bruising was forming, but she managed a smile. "Thank you."

The first man nodded. "Anything for a Guardian. My name is Isaac. This is Billy. We just happened to be around and available. Glad we could help."

Adam kept an eye on the critical patient. Zeke could tell he wasn't doing well. The leg was a goner from the knee down, at least.

They banked heavily, and Presley's eyes blinked open. He groaned and tried to roll, but Isaac put his foot on the man and held him down. Presley looked around. "Fucking cunt!"

The business end of an enormous rifle found its way directly in front of Presley's nose. "Dude, you have one choice. Shut up, never say another word in front of this woman, or die," the man named Billy said as he flipped the safety off his weapon.

Presley's eyes bulged, and his face paled, but the fucker kept his mouth shut. When they sat down at the Guardian side of the Marshall ranch, the door was opened, and Mike, plus others Zeke hadn't met, acted as litter bearers and guards. All were heavily armed, and none looked too happy to see any of the fuckers they'd taken into custody.

Zeke had only one priority. Stephanie.

"I can walk," she said half-heartedly as he carried her, trailing the rest of the people to the clinic.

"I'm not letting you out of my arms." He dropped a kiss on her head. Adam issued orders, and people scattered. "Zeke, you've got Declan and Stephanie. That way. Mike, I need you to get Ember."

"I'm here." A gorgeous redhead stepped into the main room wearing scrubs. "Maliki is going to be pissed he missed this. Guardian picked the right time to call medical conference."

"His fault he's a day late." Adam rattled off the patient information, and the woman nodded.

"OR one is ready," she said.

Zeke let the Guardians go downstairs, where he knew the operating suite was located. He carried Stephanie into the exam room upstairs. When she saw Declan lying on the table, she gasped, which made Declan jerk up into a sitting position. "Declan." Stephanie reached for her brother, and

Zeke let her stand and move to him. They clenched each other, mumbling words he couldn't make out while he gathered what he needed to tend to both Declan and Steph.

He cleaned Declan's knife wound and examined his other bruises and contusions. "Headache?"

"God, Yes," Declan admitted.

"Steph?"

"What?"

He looked over at her and smiled. "Do you have a headache, sweetheart?"

"Yeah," she admitted.

"Either one of you have nausea or feel like vomiting?" He grabbed a pen light and checked Declan's eyes.

"No." They both answered.

"Any balance problems? Dizziness? Lightheadedness? Vision problems?" Zeke went down the list as he moved between his patients. They both denied any of the obvious symptoms of a concussion. "Okay, here's the game plan. I'm going to numb your cheek and your nose."

"It's broken, isn't it?" Steph groaned when he nodded.

"Just lie down. I wish I could say this isn't going to hurt, but it will." She laid down and closed her eyes. He numbed the area and then moved over to Declan to do the same to the cheek that had been sliced. "Clean cut. This will scar, but I'll be able to minimize it."

Declan rolled his eyes. "Not like I'd win a beauty contest."

"True," Stephanie said from where she was lying down.

Declan looked over at her. "Just don't fart, Steph."

Stephanie laughed and then groaned. "Stop it, Declan."

Zeke got to work. He'd set over twenty broken noses, and the process was pretty standard. Unless it was the woman who you were in love with. He inserted a smooth instrument up her nose and applied internal and external pressure to realign the nasal bones. Zeke then inserted a nasal pack to give the bones support.

"Hey, Steph, he just put a tampon up your nose."

"Declan, I'll stitch your mouth shut," Zeke warned.

"Please, do that," Steph whispered to him.

He applied the external splint to her nose and taped everything in place. "Seven days for the nasal pack and three or four weeks for the splint."

"I'll be the talk of the town." She rolled her eyes.

"We both will be," Declan said as Zeke moved over to him.

"It could be worse." Mike White Cloud said from the doorway. "Presley Cheston, a.k.a. Paul Little, is wanted for murder."

"Drug trafficking," Stephanie said. "I took his car when I left him. He said it's full of ..."

"Fentanyl," Declan supplied for her.

"Yeah. Uncut."

"In the trunk?" Mike crossed his arms.

"No. In the frame of the car. He called it his mule."

"Where's the car now?"

"In my shed. Under a tarp." Declan said.

"I'll let the FBI know."

"FBI?" Stephanie asked.

"Federal crime, and we aren't in the position to take the lead in the investigation. They'll be here tomorrow. Do you need anything from us?"

"A ride to town when I get done here?" Zeke answered for all of them.

Mike fished in his front pocket and pulled out a set of keys. "Take my truck. The blue one with the silver toolbox in the back. It's parked by the office.

I'll get a ride into town tomorrow morning and pick it up."

"Thank you."

"You're welcome. The FBI will want to talk to both of you. Steph, you were damn smart to let Zeke know you were in trouble. Fast thinking. We're all pretty damn proud of you."

She blinked, and her bruised eyes misted up. "Thank you. May I ask a question?"

"Sure." Mike waited.

"How long will I go to jail for stealing Presley's car?"

The man smiled. "There was never a report of a stolen car. Our computer specialists confirmed it. Just tell them exactly what happened. We've got your back."

She sat quietly for a moment. "But why?"

Mike glanced at her, then at Zeke. "Because you're important to one of ours. Zeke works for us, and so do you, after a fashion. Guardian is a family, and as a family, we trust the members to keep quiet about everything they've seen and heard." He leveled a stare at both Stephanie and Declan.

The stare clicked with Declan immediately, and he quipped, "Hey, Zeke, is memory loss part of a concussion? I swear I can't remember a thing from the time I was shoveling out my truck this morning. Right, Steph?"

She looked from her brother to Mike and then at Zeke. "I must have been hit pretty hard. I can't remember a thing either."

Mike chuckled. "Except for the FBI statements and whatever story you'll tell the residents of Hollister about your injuries. You'll both be seen, so make sure your story jives."

"A helicopter landed behind my house in the field. From what you told me, two sat down at the Bit and Spur. I think a UFO blinded us on the road, and we went into the ditch."

Stephanie closed her eyes. "I'm not saying that."

"Come on. You know Edna needs something to talk about," Declan chided his sister.

Mike chuckled. "Zeke, you got your hands full with these two."

Zeke smiled. "I tell you, Mike, I'm perfectly okay with that."

21

Steph yawned heavily. After Zeke had finished stitching Declan's cheek, he was called away to work on one of Presley's men. "How much longer? I got to get to the Spur." Declan yawned.

"No, you don't. It's fine. I told you that. You need to sleep and heal." She yawned again.

Declan's stomach rumbled loudly, and Steph chuckled. "Okay, eat and then sleep."

"Ate my cupboards bare. Maybe Zeke will take us to the diner for breakfast before he takes us home." Declan contorted his face into an odd yawn, so he wouldn't stretch his jaw and pull his stitches.

"Zeke will take you to the diner, but you're both spending the day with me at my house, so I can make sure there are no complications from the knocks to the head you've taken." Zeke walked in and grabbed Chief's keys off the silver tray where he'd left them. "How are my patients?" Zeke glanced over at Declan but moved toward her. He lightly touched her cheek. "Damn, I'd go after him again if he wasn't under lock and key."

Stephanie grabbed his hand and turned it over. His knuckles were swollen, and the skin was broken. "I think he's taken enough from us."

"Yeah, I'm okay, too." Declan rolled off the table and groaned as he tried to stand straight. "Okay, maybe the Spur can wait until tomorrow."

Zeke helped her off the exam table, where she was curled up. He waited for her to get her feet. "Everyone steady?" He held her elbow and stared at Declan.

"I'll wobble, but I won't fall down. I hope." Declan shuffled to the door with Stephanie.

Once they all got in the truck and Zeke turned onto the highway, he asked. "What are you going to say happened?"

"Black ice on the way in to check the Spur. We called you, and you fixed us up and moved Dad's truck to the old shed behind the house. When the FBI takes the Mercedes with the tow truck, we can say that Steph sold it and the new owner just sent someone to pick it up." Declan said before he leaned up to the front of the double cab. "You said we can eat. Are we there yet?"

Stephanie chuckled at her brother's antics. But she was so thankful that everything had worked out. "Thank you, Zeke." She squeezed his hand as she spoke.

He looked over at her. "For what?"

"For sticking through everything last night." She didn't care if her brother heard the words.

Zeke lifted her hand and kissed it. "I'm with you, Steph. Thick or thin."

Declan grunted. "Better watch out. That sounds a lot like for better or worse."

"That doesn't scare me. I kinda like that idea." Zeke winked at her.

"Scares the hell out of me. Lord, who wants to be saddled with one woman?"

"Me." Zeke kissed her hand again, and her heart soared.

"I like that idea, too," she said to him.

"Being with a woman?" Declan laughed.

"No." Steph gave her brother a wave of her hand. "Being with one man, for better or worse." Zeke squeezed her hand after she spoke. Private communication between the two of them.

"Thank God we're almost to the diner. I'm going to be sick from all the sappy sweetness." Declan pointed. "It's open."

Zeke pulled in and helped both of them out of the truck. Steph cringed when the diner, almost full, went completely quiet. "Oh, sweet Jesus, what happened to the two of you?" Edna asked from the corner booth where she and her friends always gathered.

"Black ice, Dad's old truck went down into the ditch," Stephanie said. "It looks worse than it is."

"It looks like you went through a windshield," Edna said, scooting herself to the edge of the booth. "This booth is empty. Can I help you, Declan?" Edna waddled over and took his arm.

"Ah ... thank you." He gave Steph a look. *That* look.

"Declan ..." she warned her brother.

"I tell you, Miss Edna, I've driven on black ice all my life, but it was a brilliant flash of light that I saw that sent us into the ditch."

Edna stopped moving. "Excuse me?"

"The strangest thing. Out of nowhere, a brilliant light came up in the sky. Startled me to no end."

Declan sat down and inched his way across the booth. Stephanie did the same while shooting daggers at her brother.

"The ladies and I were discussing the sounds of helicopters last night. Couldn't see a thing, but we all heard the sounds."

Declan nodded. "Probably the feds chasing whatever it was that sent me into the ditch." He held up a hand. "Sorry, that's just me theorizing."

Edna nodded. "Makes sense. Did you hear anything when you saw that light?"

"I didn't see any lights." Stephanie pulled Edna's attention from her brother.

"Doesn't mean I didn't." Declan kept a straight face. Lord, her brother was stirring up some shit.

Zeke looked past Edna. "Hey, Ciera, would you get us three meat biscuits, whatever you have left, three cinnamon rolls, two coffees, one tea, and milk all around?"

"You got it, Doc. Sorry about the accident, Steph. Do you think you'll be able to make it to the reception tonight?"

Steph could only imagine how bad she looked, and what she wanted was food, a shower, Zeke, and a bed. In that order. "I think I'll bow out. I hope Gen likes the decorations."

"I'm sure she will. I'll get that food out to you right away. Edna, did you need more coffee?"

Edna looked back at her table. "Yes, yes, please." She patted Declan's shoulder. "We can talk more when you're feeling better."

"Sure thing. Come to the bar, and I'll buy you a beer."

"Oh ... well, it has been a long time since I've been to a bar when there wasn't an event.

"Well, you and the ladies come on by one evening. I have some really nice wines."

Edna's face blushed a vivid red. "We just may do that." She turned and glanced at Stephanie. "Honey, it's a good thing you know how to use makeup. You got two shiners that'll be with you for a while."

Laughter bubbled up, and she shook her head. "I'm not going to try to hide anything. I was in an accident. People who don't like how I look can look elsewhere."

Zeke put his arm around her, and she leaned into him. "Oh ... Oh!" Edna blinked between Zeke and Stephanie before she beamed widely. "Well, what an interesting day it is for sure. I'll let you get to your breakfast."

Ciera smiled at Edna as she moved away. Ciera lowered a tray with food and drinks to the table.

"About time," Ciera mumbled so only they could hear her.

"There's enough food here to feed an army," Stephanie exclaimed. The biscuit and cinnamon roll that Ciera put in front of her covered a salad plate each.

"I have a feeling these guys will make good use of anything you don't eat." Ciera smiled and left, moving to the diner counter to fill cups.

Stephanie leaned over, glaring at Declan. "Why?" She nodded at the booth where Edna and her hens leaned their heads together, whispering.

Declan took a big bite of his biscuit and smiled while chomping. "Because I could."

"You need to grow up," she murmured as she took a small bite of the biscuit. It was good, but her face was sore. Still, she had to put something in her stomach.

"You okay?" Zeke asked. His gaze was searching and concerned.

"Tired and sore." She smiled at him and leaned into him more. She managed to eat about half the biscuit before Declan finished it off. The milk was cold and good. She let her tea steep until the men started devouring the cinnamon rolls. It was strong, and the peppermint warmth coated her throat, sending a warm hug through her.

"Declan. Why the hell haven't you answered your phone?" Ken Zorn said from the doorway of the diner.

Declan looked at the deputy and frowned. "I think I lost it last night?" He looked at Stephanie. She nodded. It was somewhere in the wreckage of the SUV.

"What in the hell?" Ken stomped across the diner. "Sweet heavens, what in the hell happened to the two of you?"

"Dad's old truck took a spin on the black ice," Stephanie said as Ken gaped at her and then at Declan.

"Can you move?" He stared at Declan.

"I can. Why?"

"Someone broke into the Spur. The back window was smashed, and the front door was wide open."

Zeke started to say something, but Declan was moving, albeit slowly. "Steph, I thought you said it was fine yesterday?"

"It was. It had to have happened last night."

Edna popped up. "Do you think it had to do with the lights and helicopters?"

Ken looked at her. "The what? Never mind, Declan, we need to go over and find out what's missing."

Zeke spoke up. "Ken, he's been through hell. Don't let him overdo it, and bring him to my house when you're done."

"Yeah, got it." Ken opened the door for Declan, who was moving pretty fast.

Zeke took a sip of his coffee, leaned over, and whispered in her ear, "I broke in last night and took that folder off his desk."

Stephanie jerked her head up, wincing at the sudden shot of pain the abrupt movement sent down her neck and shoulders. "Shouldn't you say something?"

Zeke shook his head. "Not after that bright light bunk he was playing off to Edna."

Stephanie smiled even though it hurt. "Payback is a bitch, huh?"

"Exactly. Let's get you home." Zeke laid down enough cash to cover the bill and helped her out of the booth.

"Stephanie, if you need anything, call me," Ciera called out from the kitchen as they moved through the café.

"Steph, we're organizing a dinner train for you

and Declan for the next week. Zeke, would you be able to take it out to their place?" Edna raised her eyebrows and had a smile on her face.

Zeke nodded. "I would be honored, Edna."

"I'll be back to work in a couple of days," Stephanie argued.

"Work is one thing. Cooking when you're tired and have been working all day, that's another. Let us help. You'd do the same if it were one of us who flew through a windshield."

"Just say thank you," Zeke whispered to her as he opened the diner door.

"Thank you so much." Steph managed before tears filled her eyes. Thankfully, Zeke got her out of the diner before Edna could get out of the booth. "Thank you. I've been saying that a lot lately, haven't I?" She let Zeke help her up into Mike's truck.

"Hey, Zeke? Why do you have Mike's truck?" Carson Schmidt, the hardware store manager, said as he approached them from the direction of the store.

"Test drive. He's thinking of selling, and I'm thinking of buying."

"Another truck?" Carson asked, standing in front of the truck.

"Can never have too many trucks." Zeke waved as he got into the pickup.

"You're good at covering." Steph laid her head back against the headrest. Suddenly, it felt about twenty pounds heavier than it did earlier.

"So are you. Your brother? Not so much." Zeke chuckled and backed out into the street.

Steph hummed something and must have fallen asleep because Zeke was standing on her side of the truck the next thing she knew. "Come on. Bed for you."

Steph looked around. "You said you left your truck at the Spur."

Zeke nodded and held up a note. "Seems Mr. Browning was out for a walk and happened to see me go for a visit with our mutual friends. He brought it home for me."

"Sage?" She was still a little groggy and a whole lot tired.

"Yep. Good thing, or Ken would be arresting me for breaking and entering." Zeke held out his hand to her. "Bed."

She shook her head slowly because it hurt to move. "Shower first. I want him off me."

Zeke stopped and waited for her to look at him. "Did he ... sexually?"

Tears came to her eyes. "He didn't." He would when his temper started to wane. But when he was volatile, it was all about physical violence.

Zeke scooped her into his arms and elbowed the truck door shut. He managed to open the door to the house while carrying her, thankfully. Her stamina was gone. She *was* exhausted.

Once they were in his room, Zeke sat her on the bed and pulled off her shoes and socks. "I'll get the shower going." He hustled into the bathroom, and she heard the water turn on. She pulled off her coat and then her sweater. Blood had stained the front of it. Thank God she hadn't taken her coat off at the diner. Her bra, similarly stained, was tossed into the pile. She shimmied out of her jeans and panties.

He came out of the bathroom wearing nothing but his boxers. "Shower time." He held a hand out to her. "Come on."

She took his hand and followed him into the shower. "You should take those off."

He shook his head. "If I do, this may become something it doesn't need to be."

She stepped closer to him. "I want to feel, Zeke. Not fear, not pain, but you and me."

He removed his boxers and tossed them onto the bathroom floor. "You and me." He repeated the words and kissed her eyelids, one and the other. "I couldn't lose you. Not after just finding you."

She opened her eyes and stared up at him. "It scares me, the way I feel about you."

Zeke smiled and turned her around. "Don't get your face wet, but lean your head back." She did as he asked. He cupped the back of her head in one hand and wet her curls. She heard the snick of a shampoo bottle opening and felt the cool liquid as he poured it on. Zeke washed her hair and then her body. His hands covered her, lovingly claiming her, healing the violation that Presley had forced upon her. Zeke kissed each bruise, the three cigarette burns on her back, and finally, her swollen lips. "I feel the same way about you, Stephanie, but I'm not afraid of the feeling. Don't let anything make you afraid again. Stay here with me."

She blinked her eyes open. "You mean move in?"

"I do. I *need* you here with me. I *want* you to be with me. This thing between us is something I won't let slip away. Besides, you can't use your dad's truck. It's supposed to be totaled. I think you're stuck with me."

"That means you're stuck with me." She leaned into his chest. Her life had been a trial to this point. To Zeke. He was her home, her touchstone, and her safety. The emotions in her heart were too big to name, and she'd be terrified to try to sort them any time soon. She'd get help. Doctor Wheeler had seemed nice. She wanted to be whole for Zeke. She wanted to love him the way he deserved to be loved. In time, with Zeke, healing was possible. She knew that in her soul.

He dropped a kiss on the top of her head. "Exactly what I want. We'll get your things from Declan's tomorrow."

"I don't have much." But she was happier than she'd ever been.

"You have me, and that's enough." Zeke turned off the water while still holding her against him. "Bed."

She didn't have the willpower to argue. Zeke dried her off and carried her to bed. She felt the blanket pull up over her. "You'll always have me." Zeke's voice chased her to a dreamless sleep.

DECLAN KNOCKED on his door and hobbled in when Zeke opened it. "Anything stolen?"

"Just the file on Presley." Declan took off his coat

and toed off his boots. "Why didn't you tell me you broke into the Spur?"

Zeke shrugged. "I needed that file to give to Guardian."

"You're paying for that window. I'm not getting my insurance rates jacked up." Declan shuffled into the living room. "Where's Steph?"

"Sleeping. There are towels and some clothes for you in the hall bathroom. You've got the first room on the right."

"When will the feds be here?"

"Mike said this evening. Get clean and go to sleep."

"I'm on my way."

"Remember what I said about wound care," he reminded Declan, and the man waved him off.

"It's just a small cut."

"No, it isn't." He'd done a hell of a job stitching the man's cheek back together.

"Night." Declan entered the bathroom and shut the door.

He waited for Declan to shuffle into his bedroom and shut the door before he headed to the weight room. That was where he processed his day, where he made peace with the senseless and extinguished the occasional anger that found him. Today, he had a body full of rage. Rage at Presley and everything the man represented.

Zeke pushed himself, knowing sleep wouldn't come until he worked through what happened last night. The righteousness he felt in beating Presley. Righteousness that he should never covet, but that one time, he would.

His cell rang, and he picked it up. The name on the screen made him smile. "Hey, Mom."

"Hey yourself. Are you too snowed in to call your mom and tell her you're alive?"

"Mom, I'm alive." He chuckled. "Sorry, things have been hectic around here. You know how that goes."

"Well, I would if my boy would call and fill me in." There was a pause. "Did that work? Do you feel guilty?"

He laughed. "Not in the slightest."

"Dang it. Pete told me it wouldn't." His mom sighed. "How bad was the storm?"

"It was epic. We just got the roads cleared yesterday."

"You should move to Florida," she said matter-of-factly.

"And deal with hurricanes? No, thank you."

"You'd rather deal with tornadoes, locusts, hail, and snowstorms?"

"I don't recall any locust swarms." He laughed at her.

"Fine. Fill me in on the gossip."

"One of the locals is trying to get Edna back on the UFO trail."

"Really? Is she going to buy it?"

"I'm not sure. It sounded like she was taking the bait this morning."

"How are things up there?" Her attempt at finding out if he was seeing anyone.

Zeke didn't answer as a smile spread across his face. "What!" she squealed. "What is her name?"

"Stephanie."

"Such a lovely name. What does she do?"

"She works in the clinic with me."

"A doctor or a nurse?"

"A receptionist."

"Perfect!" He felt his mom would have said the same thing if he had told her that Stephanie was the janitor.

"Tell me all about her," she half pleaded, half begged.

"Well, she's got the kindest heart." Zeke leaned

back against the wall and got comfortable. The call could be a long one.

ZEKE OPENED his bedroom door quietly. After talking to his mom for almost an hour, he showered again in the hall bathroom, then went to bed. He'd be able to get four hours before they'd need to wake up. He'd set the alarm on his phone. With care, he climbed into bed and snuggled up behind Stephanie. She backed into him and formed her frame to his body. Her head lifted, and she stared at the clock on the nightstand. "Are you just coming to sleep?"

He pulled her back into him. "Shhh … Go back to sleep.

"No." She reached back and circled his cock with her hand.

Five strokes, and he was growing, primed, and ready. "You need your sleep."

Stephanie hushed him and wiggled her hips. She lifted her leg over his legs and used her hand to guide him into her. "Slow," she whispered the words as he pushed into her and then retreated. God, she was hot and so fucking tight. He rocked his way inside her core. He kissed her shoulder and fondled her breasts the way she liked as he continued to rock inside her. Lifting on his elbow, he lifted her leg and held it higher. The slide of his cock inside her was heaven. Her heat enveloped him and then released. The sensations were so vivid he was blinded to anything but them. He felt her tighten, and her hips pushed back against him. He drove home harder, barely registering that his headboard was pounding against the wall. He let that thought slip away with everything else as he released inside her. He dropped down behind her and pulled her toward him.

"I think we may have woken your brother." Zeke nuzzled past her curls and kissed the side of her neck.

Stephanie laughed softly and yawned. She grabbed his arm and wrapped it around her. "Good. Payback is a bitch."

22

Stephanie shut the door to the truck she'd bought two months ago and hurried into the Spur. She was late getting back, but she'd learned so much from Dori that they'd stayed late. The sun was warm, and the trees and grass were that vibrant shade of green that only spring could produce. As she walked into the bar, she let her eyes adjust to the darkness. "Hi, Phil. How are you doing?" she greeted as she passed.

"Doing." He lifted the beer he had every day after work and saluted her.

She laughed and spoke to people crowded into the bar as she headed to the far end where Zeke sat. "Wow, there are a lot of people here today." She stopped by Zeke, and he got off the stool he was sitting on, offering it to her after getting a kiss. She was so in love with Zeke that it hurt. He was the most amazing man. "Thank you. What's going on?"

Zeke looked around. "Not much. Seems like everyone had the same idea as we did."

Declan brought her a glass of beer. "Hey, I got Dad's truck running."

Stephanie turned away from Zeke. "You did? That's wonderful." Although it wasn't wrecked the night they said it was, the engine died about a week later. Declan had been tinkering with it since. "Isn't that—" She turned around, looking for Zeke. He was … on his knee.

There wasn't a sound in the bar. Not a sound. "Stephanie Howard, will you marry me?"

Stephanie felt her hands over her mouth, although she had no idea how they got there. She knew she was nodding but couldn't make herself say the words.

"Is that a yes?" Zeke smiled and reached for her left hand.

"Yes! God, Yes. I love you." She wrapped her arms around his neck as soon as he put the ring on her finger.

She was in his arms and spinning around to the sound of thunderous applause. She held on to the man who had put her back together, piece by piece. The man she'd fallen head over heels in love with during a snowstorm, and the man who would be her future, her foundation, and would always be her salvation.

DECLAN SERVED beer on the house. His little sister was worth the cost. He watched as she glowed in happiness next to his friend. They were perfect for each other. Perfect together. He turned as the door to the bar opened. He recognized the face. Melody something or another. She was one of the few women with whom he'd had repeat performances. She was a hellcat in bed. He put a beer in front of her, but she shook her head. Her long brown hair fell over her shoulder.

He leaned closer to be heard over the laughter and talking happening in the bar. "Something stronger?"

She glanced at all the people. To be honest, it was a packed house. She leaned over the bar, her breasts on full display. "No. When do you close?"

"Tonight? Probably midnight. You want to meet me at my place?" He waggled his eyebrows.

"Yeah. That's probably better."

"Better than what?" Declan laughed.

Melody shook her head and mouthed, "See you tonight."

He winked at her and headed back down the bar to pull more beer from the tap. He was going to have some wildcat sex tonight.

The End.

ALSO BY KRIS MICHAELS

Kings of the Guardian Series

Jacob: Kings of the Guardian Book 1

Joseph: Kings of the Guardian Book 2

Adam: Kings of the Guardian Book 3

Jason: Kings of the Guardian Book 4

Jared: Kings of the Guardian Book 5

Jasmine: Kings of the Guardian Book 6

Chief: The Kings of Guardian Book 7

Jewell: Kings of the Guardian Book 8

Jade: Kings of the Guardian Book 9

Justin: Kings of the Guardian Book 10

Christmas with the Kings

Drake: Kings of the Guardian Book 11

Dixon: Kings of the Guardian Book 12

Passages: The Kings of Guardian Book 13

Promises: The Kings of Guardian Book 14

The Siege: Book One, The Kings of Guardian Book 15

The Siege: Book Two, The Kings of Guardian Book 16

A Backwater Blessing: A Kings of Guardian Crossover Novella

Montana Guardian: A Kings of Guardian Novella

Guardian Defenders Series

Gabriel

Maliki

John

Jeremiah

Frank

Guardian Security Shadow World

Anubis (Guardian Shadow World Book 1)

Asp (Guardian Shadow World Book 2)

Lycos (Guardian Shadow World Book 3)

Thanatos (Guardian Shadow World Book 4)

Tempest (Guardian Shadow World Book 5)

Smoke (Guardian Shadow World Book 6)

Reaper (Guardian Shadow World Book 7)

Phoenix (Guardian Shadow World Book 8)

Valkyrie (Guardian Shadow World Book 9)

Hollister (A Guardian Crossover Series)

Andrew (Hollister-Book 1)

Zeke (Hollister-Book 2)

Hope City

Hope City - Brock

HOPE CITY - Brody- Book 3

Hope City - Ryker - Book 5

Hope City - Killian - Book 8

Hope City - Blayze - Book 10

The Long Road Home

Season One:

My Heart's Home

Season Two:

Searching for Home (A Hollister-Guardian Crossover Novel)

STAND ALONE NOVELS

SEAL Forever - Silver SEALs

A Heart's Desire - Stand Alone

Hot SEAL, Single Malt (SEALs in Paradise)

Hot SEAL, Savannah Nights (SEALs in Paradise)

Hot SEAL, Silent Knight (SEALs in Paradise)

ABOUT THE AUTHOR

Wall Street Journal and USA Today Bestselling Author, Kris Michaels is the alter ego of a happily married wife and mother. She writes romance, usually with characters from military and law enforcement backgrounds.

Made in United States
Orlando, FL
24 October 2022

23794243R00163